Spoon

Spoon

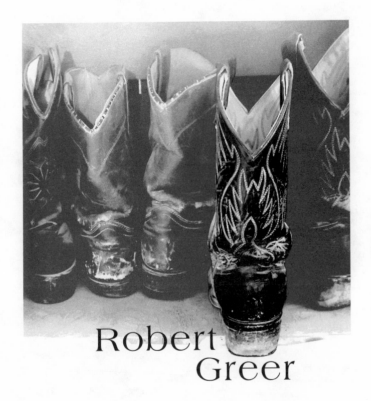

Robert
Greer

FULCRUM
GOLDEN, COLORADO

Library of Congress Cataloging-in-Publication Data

Greer, Robert O.
  Spoon / Robert Greer.
    p. cm.
  ISBN 978-1-55591-689-3 (hardcover)
  1. Indians--Mixed descent--Fiction. 2. Ranchers--Fiction. 3. Ranch life--Fiction. 4. Montana--Fiction. I. Title.
  PS3557.R3997S66 2009
  813'.54--dc22

                    2009014558

Printed in the United States of America by Malloy Inc.
0 9 8 7 6 5 4 3 2 1

Design by Jack Lenzo

Fulcrum Publishing
4690 Table Mountain Drive, Suite 100
Golden, Colorado 80403
www.fulcrumbooks.com

Again and Always
for Phyllis

One

A year ago this past August, on the outskirts of Hardin, Montana, riding along I-90 on the crest of a warm downslope summer wind, I picked up a hitchhiker wearing a $250 5X beaver Resistol cowboy hat and no shoes. He told me his name was Spoon. TJ Darley, I told him in return. His hat was snow white with a Tom Mix block, and he wore it tipped forward just enough to shade his eyes. When I asked him what had happened to his shoes, he winked, looked deeply reflective, and said, "Shoes can be excess baggage when a man's in a hurry."

A mile or so of silence later, he told me he was a part-black, part-Indian cowboy searching for his roots and that he'd just been fired from a ranch eighty miles back down the road. Pensively drinking in the landscape, he added that he was hungry, and if we ran over a jackrabbit, we could build a fire and roast it on a stick. I nodded without responding, now surveying the countryside I'd known all my life just as intently as Spoon. When a jackrabbit popped up along the shoulder and Spoon yelled, "Hit that long-legged s-o-b!" I knew with certainty he meant every word.

Hardin is Custer country. Rolling grasslands and sagebrush-covered hills rim the town and the green river valley where the golden-haired general made his final stand, and the Rosebud Mountains rise in the distance, highlighting the site of America's final Indian war. On wind-silent, ice-clear summer days, when the sky is gemstone blue and a few orphaned alabaster clouds hang motionless overhead, you can look from the western bluffs that border the fourteen thousand acres of my family's Willow Creek Ranch and see the Custer battlefield monument rising from the Bighorn riverbank in the northern distance. Those are the days that make me wonder how my dad will keep the whole thing going.

The animal-centered ranch he grew up with has become a thing of the past. Modern ranches are nothing more than machines for feeding cows. He can't hire anybody who cares enough about mechanical work or irrigation to do either one right, and God knows he never planned to count on me. He says I dream too much, like every second son. My mom, the glue and buffer between us, accommodates us both in her own special way as we reach the climax of a Montana ranch land culture that's fading like ripples in a stream.

Brown eyes gleaming, Spoon twisted toward me in his seat and eyed me pointedly. The sun-baked vinyl squeaked as he relaxed and tipped his hat back. "Got any idea where there might be a job for a first-class hand?"

"What are you good at?"

"Anything to do with cattle, but calvin's my thing."

I shuddered, thinking of all the icy winter nights I'd

slept in our calving barn tending a mother cow trying to calve, recalling the helpless times I'd lost one of them, or both.

"Are you a chain puller or a wait-and-see kinda man?" I asked.

"Never used a chain to pull an animal in my life. Would you want somebody usin' a chain to yank you into this world?"

Spoon paused, looking for my response, then took right off again.

"I talk to an animal real soft and sugar sweet, or maybe use Spoon's 'gentle persuasion,' but never no chains. Mostly I trust my head and my hands."

He shoved his callused palms my way and turned them from side to side. The backs of his hands were cocoa brown and surprisingly butter smooth.

"How are you at irrigation?" I asked, following the curve of the interstate.

"Not bad, but like I said, birthin's my game."

"Have you ever heard of Willow Creek Ranch?"

"Can't say that I have."

When he leaned back against the truck's door and stroked the midline cleft in his chin, I noticed that his forearms were long and muscular, his upper torso solid looking and lean.

"We might have something for you there."

"Do you own the place?" he asked, looking puzzled.

"No, but my folks do."

"Then you don't have no job to offer." Spoon tipped his hat back down over his eyes and smiled. "But take me to the source. You never know, I might be able to do your folks some good."

My dad brought my mom to the Willow Creek valley from New York at the end of the Korean War. They'd been married for only sixty-five days. She had been a June Taylor Dancer, the tallest in the original pretelevision troupe of seventeen. My dad had been a navy Seabee and demolitions expert stationed somewhere in the Sea of Japan. Back then, he was a teller of tales. My mom says his stories all had a dash of yeast added to allow them to rise.

One of his best, the one my mom claims first sparked her interest, detailed how long before Korea he'd gotten into demolitions. He told my mom that during the early 1900s, his grandfather had been a leading Montana citizen intent on building a half-million-acre cattle empire on the banks of the Little Bighorn. In doing so, his granddad created his share of enemies, so he built a ranch house in which every room had an outside door, and the dining room offered views in all directions. A panel beside the living room fireplace led to an underground hideaway connected to a tunnel running two hundred yards west. According to my dad, my grandfather kept ten sticks of dynamite in a ventilation pipe in an underground room. If enemies were to enter the house, a family member had instructions to bang on the bedroom floor with a broomstick. Moving to the room below, my grandfather would then light a stick of dynamite with an extra-long fuse. Then he would ring a cowbell, a signal for his family and allies to vacate the house, and leave himself just enough time to crawl through the tunnel to an outbuilding where he would quickly saddle a horse, ready to fly.

My parents traveled first class by train on the El Capitan from New York to Montana in the spring of 1954. When my mom saw the original Willow Creek homestead, a two-room mud-and-split-log cabin surrounded by two hundred fifty acres of chickweed and sage, she refused to eat for three full days.

My brother, Jimmy, was born in 1954. He died trying to swim across Willow Creek in 1969. When Jimmy died, my dad's far-fetched tales smoldered to an end. For a while the ranch filled the void, but soon he soured and let the land temporarily drift to seed. I was born in 1972, a midlife replacement, too late to resurrect his fire. In the nineteen years since, his bitterness has reached the point of raspy-voiced distrust.

△ △ △

The sun was setting, its slow arc west nearly complete, when I eased my shortbed truck up to our ranch house's back door. I left Spoon sitting in the pickup, promising him that if I couldn't get him a job, I'd at least round up a pair of shoes for him. I stepped into the darkened mudroom and tripped over a cluster of widemouthed Mason jars filled with wild blackberries that my mom had picked earlier that afternoon. The sound of breaking glass echoed through the room.

"Bill Darley, if you broke the skin on a single blackberry, I'll have your head!" my mom called from the kitchen.

"I'm gonna need a broom. There's been a berry disaster out here," I said, scooping up a handful of blackberries from a nearby bowl and stepping into the warm glow of my mom's kitchen.

"TJ, I thought you were your dad. I didn't hear you drive up."

"I drifted in on the wind," I said with a smile.

"Well, drift back out there and clean up your mess." She handed me a dustpan and broom.

I popped a couple of blackberries into my mouth, went back to the mudroom, and began cleaning up. "I've found someone I think can help with calving and maybe irrigation too," I called.

"I'm not the one you need to convince," she said, her voice straining as it always did when it came to making decisions about the ranch.

"He'll have to hire someone, or sooner or later we'll go under. The place is too much for the three of us to handle alone."

She came into the mudroom, looked right through me, and said, "He's stubborn, TJ."

"So was Custer."

When she brought an index finger up gently across her lips, I knew not to say another word.

Spoon was sitting on the tailgate of my truck, hunched over, knees beneath his chin, massaging his feet when we came out of the house. It was nearly dark. Next to the truck, a stand of aspen rustled in the breeze. The instant he caught sight of my mom, he jumped to the ground and took off his hat.

"Arcus Witherspoon," he said.

"I'm Marva Darley," my mom said, placing the same forceful emphasis on both names, as was her custom. "You're an irrigating and calving man, I understand."

As she eyed his shoeless feet, Spoon shot me a look that told me he wondered what else I might have said while I was inside.

"Mr. Witherspoon, if you don't mind my asking, do you irrigate with or without your shoes?"

"It's Spoon, ma'am, and I can do it either way."

"And calving?"

"Always take special care with mothers and their babies. It's the only way."

My mom smiled, gave me a thumbs-up sign, and said, "Convince your dad."

Spoon sat back down on the tailgate, looking self-satisfied.

"Nice meeting you, Mr. Witherspoon." She was half-way to the house when she turned back to me. "Run over to the tack room and get Mr. Witherspoon some boots, TJ."

I smiled and waved for Spoon to follow me.

Once a horseman's jewel, the neglected tack room had been in decline since Jimmy's death. Mom called the room one of my dad's confusions. It was a twenty-five-by-twenty-five-foot heat-trapping hot box connected by a breezeway to a decaying bunkhouse that hadn't been used in twenty years. Yellowing boxcar siding made up the interior walls, and years of spur tracks had bruised almost every inch of floor. A hodgepodge of aging saddles, all in need of repair, hugged several rickety sawhorses scattered around the room, and badly weathered bridles had been looped over several wall-bracing two-by-fours. Mildewed heaps of saddle blankets and rugs were lumped on either side of the door, and boots, some still caked to the heel scallops with dried mud, lined every wall.

Spoon, taking in the scene and getting his bearings, immediately gathered half a dozen boots, sat down side-saddle on an unsteady sawhorse, and began trying them on one by one. "What's a man need with all these shoes?" he asked, shaking his head as he tugged on a fancy-looking tricolored boot with inlaid jingle bobs. He struggled to free his foot with a loud grunt, and the boot fell to the floor, jingle bobs ringing.

"Boots just seem to accumulate in here," I said. "Hired hands leave 'em behind. People outgrow 'em. The ones over there in the corner—the ones that look almost new—those belonged to my brother, Jimmy. A few around here are even mine."

"That sucker I just tried on pinched like heck," said Spoon, shaking his head and tugging on another boot. "Too big," he sighed, tossing it aside. Quickly he tried on three or four more, each time frowning at the fit.

While Spoon continued trying on boots, I walked over to the musty pile of saddle blankets, nudging them with my toe, then knelt and began smoothing out a frayed Indian blanket with an intricate zigzag design. Just as my thumb punched through a raveling moth hole, Spoon yelled, "Damn, these fit!" He jumped off the sawhorse, admiring the pair of run-over boots and grinning broadly.

"Let me have a look."

He walked over to me proudly, long arms swinging at his sides. The boots were rough-cut cowhide, and the leather was cracked from heel to toe. On the right boot, a worn leather strap held on a tarnished silver spur.

"Those belonged to a buckaroo. All you need now are chinks and a fancy silver bit for your horse," I said, forcing back a smile.

"Means these didn't belong to no real cowboy," Spoon said, looking disappointed.

"You're right there," I said, knowing that real cowboys favor full-length chaps and never sport silver, while a buckaroo is what you might call a sorta cowboy yuppie.

Spoon nodded, jiggled his pants down over the boot tops, and walked around the room, testing out the fit. "Nice, real nice."

After half a dozen circles around the room, Spoon eased back onto the sawhorse and stretched out his right leg. The spur spun counterclockwise in the musty air.

"Thanks," he said, bending down and tracing one of the scores of spur tracks in the soft pine floor with his thumb. For a while there was silence, except for the sound of the two of us breathing and the outside howl of the wind.

"Know how I lost my shoes?" asked Spoon, sitting up straight and admiring the boots.

"Haven't got a clue."

He stood up and eased the sawhorse back against the wall. Like the legs on a newborn colt, all four of the sawhorse's legs wobbled out of sync. In a tired, sullen, day's-end kind of voice, Spoon whispered, "Playin' cards. And to make matters worse, I lost 'em to a couple of down-and-out

Crows." His voice rose an octave. "I don't particularly like Crows. The s-o-bs scouted for Custer, and, to top it off, they let white folks saddle 'em with dumb-ass names."

He looked at me for confirmation, but I didn't say a word.

"Well, they did. Still do," he said. "Would you let anybody stick you with a moniker like White Man Runs Him or Firewater Lover or Chicken Heart?"

I shook my head.

"The mistake I made was tellin' them two Crows up front I was part Cheyenne. There's no love lost between us Cheyenne and the Crow, you know. One of 'em even said to me while he was dealin' that I looked more like some bug-eyed colored boy than any Indian he'd ever seen. I bit my tongue, like I always do to check my temper, reached in my back pocket, pulled out my wallet, and showed the Crows my tribal card. All real Indians carry a card, you know," Spoon said, proudly slipping a card from his wallet and handing it to me to emphasize his point.

I flipped the Bureau of Indian Affairs blue card from side to side and handed it back.

"Those two Crows looked my card over, just like you. The one who'd called me bug-eyed let out one of those so-what kinda grunts, and the next thing ya know, we were playin' Texas Hold 'Em and drinkin' 151-proof rum like long-lost friends. Forty-five minutes later I was up a hundred and a half. About then the other Crow, a fancy dancer who claimed he'd won hundreds of dance competitions on reservations all over the West, started to cheat. I caught him turnin' the edges of his cards so he could watch for 'em on the next deal. When I called him on it, the fancy-dancin' bastard pulled a knife. Next thing I knew, his buddy was down on all fours, pullin' at my feet. By the time they left they had my boots, my belt, my socks, and the last ninety bucks I had in this world. Yes, indeed. They left, and so did I."

Looking sullen, Spoon pulled a miniature tenth of Bacardi, the kind the airlines hand out, from his shirt pocket, uncapped it, and handed the bottle and cap to me. I hesitantly took a swallow, recapped the bottle, and handed it back. As he slipped half a dozen more from his pockets and lined them up in front of us on the floor, I had the sense we were navigating the edges of a special occasion and that drinking wasn't something Spoon normally did. In the next half hour, as we went through the bottles, I learned that Spoon had been an eighteen-year-old aft-deck machine gunner on an assault support patrol boat that had cruised the Mekong River during the Vietnam War. He had lost a half brother and a cousin during the war and had been drifting ever since.

"I wore my hair short during 'Nam. My chief would shit a brick if he saw me now," Spoon said, uncapping a new bottle and tugging at his thick, coarse, almost-shoulder-length hair. Hair that seemed too abundant for his narrow face and lean, shorter-than-six-foot frame. "I read a lot of Malcolm X on them river floats and pissed and moaned the whole while that come separation day I was headed back to the States to do two things: find my roots and get my rights. But after Cisco and my cousin Davey-Boy got killed, I sorta lost my way. For three years after Vietnam,

'71 through '74, I drank. Drank like a brain-dead wino, some folks said. When I wasn't drinkin' I was driftin' and tellin' anybody wantin' to know that I was tracin' my roots. The only thing I knew about my family, besides us bein' what they call half-and-half back where I come from, was that my great-grandfather had supposedly been part of a band of freedmen who'd filed homestead claims in Kansas about 1878."

Brown eyes gleaming and with an obvious buzz, Spoon walked over to the rug and saddle-blanket pile. In the dim light and under the spell of the rum, he looked taller than when he'd first sat down, but in truth he was no more than five foot eleven, a couple of inches or so shorter than me.

"You shouldn'ta let the moths get to this one," he said, tugging at the corner of the blanket I'd straightened out earlier. "It's a pretty rare turn-of-the-century Navajo weave. Without the holes, it would bring eighteen hundred bucks, easy."

"I'll talk to my dad about it," I said, eager for Spoon to finish his story.

He fanned the blanket out on the floor, sat on it, and, legs crossed Indian-style, making sure his boots never touched the decaying wool, cleared his throat and continued, "There's an all-black town in Kansas called Nicodemus. Three days short of turnin' twenty-five, I met an old woman sellin' sweet corn at a roadside stand outside town. Her silver hair hung to the small of her back in two long, thick braids, and it was pretty obvious from the way her teeth clicked together when she talked that she wore dentures. Dentures that were too big, 'cause the old woman's face was fixed into a constant smile. While we dickered on the price of the corn, I mentioned my name and told her I was tracin' my roots. She said she'd known my granddad, even laughed and called him a woolly headed rascal with a fancy for Indian women, finally mentioning that he'd married a Cheyenne woman who had the *charm*."

I frowned, unfamiliar with the term.

With an index finger Spoon spelled out c-h-a-r-m in midair. "My grandmother could see things," he said with a wink.

When I still didn't comprehend, Spoon threw up his hands and rolled his eyes. "She could see into the future, TJ. Don't you know nothin' at all?"

"Oh, sure," I said, nodding as Spoon readjusted himself on the rug.

We finished the last of the Bacardi a few minutes later, and I told Spoon he could sleep in the bunkhouse that night.

"No need for me to move in there," Spoon said, looking toward the darkened corridor that led to the old bunkhouse. "This pile of blankets'll do just fine." He patted the blankets, sending ribbons of dust into the air.

I left him sitting on the rug, pulling off his boots, proud that I'd been the Darley who'd made the decision that, at least for the time being, Spoon would stay.

As I walked back to our house in darkness, I found myself wondering what it was that drove a man like Spoon, and then wondering even more what it was that drove me.

Spoon seemed intent on tracing down his roots, and I expected that in the long run he most certainly would.

I, on the other hand, had no real sense of what I was chasing. I'd finished high school more than a year earlier and passed up a scholarship to study agriscience and geology at the University of Montana, choosing instead to help at the ranch. In some ways, I knew I was hiding. Hiding from moving ahead and running headlong into life's necessary but often untidy decisions. Hiding from the fact that I would always be Jimmy Darley's athletically gifted but far-too-bookish kid brother.

Spoon seemed to know clear enough who he was, but not where he'd come from. I knew precisely where I'd come from, but far too little about who I really was, where I was going, or who I might become. My mom had always dreamed I'd become a veterinarian. Dad's greatest hope, it had always seemed to me, unlike the hopes and dreams he'd had for Jimmy, was that I'd simply be self-sufficient.

As I paused and gazed skyward, I wondered how many enemy soldiers Spoon had killed during Vietnam and if his odyssey to find his roots and connect with his soul was simply a way of staving off some terrible darkness in his past, the same way I was likely doing by holding the future at bay.

When I looked back to see if the lights inside the tack room were still on, the windows were dark. I could make out the shape of the fur-sided old building easy enough as moonlight reflected off its corrugated metal roof, but there was no hint that anyone was inside. Yet even in the darkness, I could feel Spoon's presence, imagine him breathing, see his incisive, deep-set eyes and weathered brown skin. He was there all right, and I had the strange sudden sense that he'd become a guidepost for me.

Two

My dad, short necked and broad from my angle, with just barely sloping shoulders and a thick mop of sandy blond hair, identical to mine, was the do-it-yourself-or-not-at-all kind of person who had no use for hired men. He argued that most of them didn't like their work and that any man who hated his work probably disliked himself even more. When I was ten, a hired man ran my dad's best cutting horse into a snowbank and shattered her leg. Dad put the big mare down with a single shot above the ear. Later, another hand, a man Dad had known and trusted for years, stole the Willow Creek tally book during the summer, made a duplicate, clipped out a couple of pages for himself, altered our Triangle Long Bar brand, and shorted us fifteen yearlings at auction that fall. Dad broke the man's leg with a branding iron when he found out, but he never got back the money the yearlings brought. So I knew I'd be up against it when I came to him with my recommendation to take on a new hand.

The mountain air was unusually humid the morning I asked my dad to hire Spoon. A late-summer fog had settled over the heifer meadow pond and along the lane leading up to our house, and from our kitchen I could see a group of five mother cows brushing against one another looking sleepy-eyed. I wondered how Spoon had slept and whether, during the unseasonably chilly night, he'd been forced to wrap himself in one of the moth-eaten Navajo blankets.

"He's a con man," my dad said as we ate breakfast. "Nowadays they almost always are." He bolted down a spoonful of the cornbread he'd crunched up in a Mason jar filled with buttermilk.

"I don't think so," said Mom. "I'd at least give him a try, Bill."

"So he can sucker punch us for five hundred a month plus room and board? No way."

"He'd sure be a help with our second alfalfa cutting, and I could use a hand riding fence the rest of the year," I said.

"We can do those things ourselves. No need hirin' 'em out."

I looked over at my mom. The look in her eyes told me not to push too hard. "Give him a trial, a month or two. It won't break us, Bill," she said.

"It'll shove us a damn sight closer to the poorhouse, that's all."

"At least talk to the man," I said, knowing that my dad's assertion was really an exaggeration. "He's willing to give us a try. That's more than most locals'll do."

Dad flashed me a debate-ending stare, the kind he saved for those times when he'd reached his limit. "Local folks know what I pay and what I expect if they decide to hire on here. This ranch is laid out for family, not driftin' ranch hands."

When the thin, eight-inch scar that ran down his left cheek, a scar he'd had since Korea, turned salmon pink, the way it tended to do when he was about to lose control, I knew it was time to end the argument.

My mom walked over and smoothed down the collar of his rumpled chambray shirt. Her long, delicate hands, hands that matched her slender, graceful, athletic frame, slipped onto his shoulders, then down his arms, until they met his massive, weathered hands. Rubbing them gently, she said, "He's an extra body, and he's willing, Bill. The three of us can't continue to manage six hundred cows. There's no way we can keep running against the wind forever."

Dad stirred his spoon slowly around in the Mason jar until the buttermilk and cornbread turned to the thick, gummy mixture he enjoyed. He drank half of it before setting the jar aside. "Does he know one damn thing about ranchin'?"

"He says he does."

"We'll see." As he stood up and adjusted his belt, my dad's right knee buckled, giving way as it did a couple of times a week. Before he could straighten back up, my mom had her arm hooked through his, and she began slowly walking him toward the door. "We'll see," he said again.

I winked at my mom and followed.

Even with mom softening him up, my dad would never have hired Spoon if we hadn't so desperately the needed help, and, of course, there was Spoon's bet.

Spoon told my dad as part of their negotiations that morning, with my mom and I standing right there on our front porch as they talked, that he could cut a one-hundred-eighty-acre field of alfalfa and tame hay, five-string-bale the cuttings, pick up the bales from the field, and stack them neat as a pin, all within twenty-four hours. My dad said it was impossible, insisting that the alfalfa couldn't possibly even cure in that short a time, but agreeing just the same that if Spoon could come within four hours of the twenty-four-hour limit, he had himself a job. Spoon's only requests before starting were that we give him five quart jugs of water, that he be allowed to start after dusk, and that we flood the field with light.

At eight thirty that evening, my dad had our two backhoes sitting catty-corner from one another at either end of the field, diesel engines humming, headlight beams on high. I'd centered a John Deere 350 Junior we used for cutting the grass around the house along the fence line at midfield with its lights on. Across from the tractor, fifty yards away on the other side of the field, I'd lined up my pickup and snapped on the headlights before racing to where my dad sat in one of the backhoes.

At eight forty-five sharp, Spoon pulled onto the northern edge of the brightly lit field in our red and green McCormick with duals, pulling a twenty-year-old swather and kicking up a trail of dust. He parked next to the backhoe my dad was sitting in. His face was wrapped in a white bandanna pulled up to within an inch of his eyes. In the glare of the headlights and with streams of dust rising in the air, he looked like a heavy-metal rock musician ascending in a dry-ice mist from below center stage to begin his act.

"Twenty-eight hours!" shouted my dad above the hum of the idling engines, looking up at Spoon. "Four hours are on me!"

"I only asked for twenty-four!" hollered Spoon. "But I'll take the extra!" He nudged the tractor into gear. It lurched forward, clanking over a cattle guard before heading out into the field.

△ △ △

Spoon stopped for his second quart of water the next morning just before eight. By then three-quarters of the field had been leveled, and the freshly mown alfalfa was drying in the morning sun. When he cut the tractor's engine, the air, which had been surprisingly still until that moment, was suddenly filled with a twenty-miles-per-hour hay-drying wind. Mulling over where the wind had come from, I listened to the sad call of half a dozen mourning doves looking down on us from the telephone wires along the county road.

Although I had stayed all night to watch Spoon, my dad had watched him for less than ten minutes before leaving. From the bed of my pickup, I watched as Spoon undid his bandanna and wiped the sweat from around his neck. Somehow Spoon and the tractor and the swather looked smaller than they had the night before, as if I were seeing them through the wrong end of a pair of binoculars.

What if Spoon couldn't finish? I asked myself. *The way Jimmy couldn't finish swimming across Willow Creek?* My dad had told Jimmy not to try, warned him that no one could swim across Willow Creek at high water. But, just like now, he hadn't been there when Jimmy had tried.

Since then my dad's victories had always seemed to be the melancholy kind that came from knowing he was right.

The tractor's engine kicked back on, a loud belch of black diesel exhaust rose in the air, and Spoon's bandanna was back over his face. Moments later a new row of alfalfa began dropping in the swather's wake. The morning sun had heated the pickup's bed to the point that I could feel the warm corrugated metal through my jeans. I stood and stretched, impeded momentarily by knotted muscles and calf cramps. The sweet molasses smell of freshly cut alfalfa filled the air as I watched Spoon continue. A little before ten thirty, when I backed the pickup from the field edge onto the county road to leave, Spoon was cutting the last row of alfalfa next to the quarter-section fence. I stopped on the road, got out, and waved at him, crossing my arms back and forth above my head. I didn't think he saw me, but when I eased the truck into gear moments later, "Shave and a Haircut" echoed from the tractor's horn.

I spent the rest of the day repairing a broken head-gate on our number four irrigation ditch and plowing under ten acres of dryland meadow we'd lost to gophers and sage. It was close to five before I got back to Spoon. He was midfield, baling four-by-six-foot bales of hay. I couldn't imagine how the alfalfa had cured enough for him to bale, but it had, and I had the sense that he'd known all along it would. The wind kicked up, dusting my windshield with pollen as I bumped across the shallow tractor ruts Spoon had left in the freshly mown field. Spoon still had to stack the hay onto a flatbed semitrailer parked near the end of the field, but if he finished baling by seven I knew he stood a chance. It was then that I realized he was at least as determined as my dad.

By the time Spoon started stacking, it was nearly dark. A full moon, tractor and backhoe lights, and my pickup's high beams were his only sources of light. He'd passed in front of me and nodded when I'd first switched on my lights, but he hadn't said a word. The lowboy hay loader he was using had been around the ranch for close to thirty years. Metal grated against metal each time the loader uncradled another four bales onto the flatbed, and I wondered whether each trip back to the field with the temperamental loader would be Spoon's last.

My dad showed up just before eight, his battered long-necked flashlight swinging at his side. Spoon topped off the flatbed's twelve-foot-high hay crown at 8:22. He climbed down from the neatly stacked bales, puffy faced, his skin a muddy river-bottom brown. Hay welts crisscrossed his arms, and alfalfa pollen had stained his bandanna golden brown. Out of the blue he tossed me his sweat-stained hat, and I saw a three-inch ring of moist, caked-up salt circling the crown.

"I could use some water," he said, out of breath. "Ran out a little before five." He reached up onto the lip of the flatbed and handed me one of his jugs. I ran for my pickup to fill it from my thermos. When I returned, Spoon was lying on the ground on his back. He rested his head on a pillow of loose alfalfa. My dad stood a couple of feet away, leaning on one corner of the semitrailer; his flashlight, wedged between two hay bales, shone up into the sky.

"I figured you'd make it when I drove by about six," he said, looking down at a motionless Spoon. "I guess I gauged it pretty close."

Spoon didn't answer.

"Five hundred a month and board," said my dad.

"Six," said Spoon, his voice floating up from the ground.

My dad hesitated a moment, nodded, grabbed his flashlight, and walked away.

Spoon raised himself and leaned against one of the semi's tires. Resting his head against the greasy hub, he looked at me and said, "Pour that water over my face, TJ." I smiled as I splashed water down over his head onto his face and into his ears.

"How about another jugful?" he asked softly, shaking his head back and forth like a wet puppy shedding water in the summer sun. Still smiling, I ran for the truck. On the return trip, the fact that we finally had some help began to sink in.

◁ ◁ ◁

By Thanksgiving, Spoon was settled in. The old tack room and bunkhouse bore his stamp. He had stripped, sanded, and polyurethaned the floors to a golden, mirror-gloss finish. Several wood-framed Indian blankets hung from the tack-room walls, and a five-point antelope head, one I'd helped him hang, jutted from above the room's potbellied stove.

He had a routine. He dutifully picked up his job

ticket at six in the morning each workday and worked six days straight before leaving the ranch each Saturday night to go to town. My mom claimed he gambled. Dad said he drank. Whatever his vice, we hardly ever saw Spoon until midday Sunday, his one day off.

He and my dad didn't talk much, and when they did, their conversations always had to do with work. Spoon usually ate alone. On those rare occasions when he did take his meals with us, my mom would usually ease the tension, talking about the weather, growing blackberries, and canning, or recalling the times in New York when she used to dance. Spoon always ate fast, rarely looked up, and excused himself as soon as he was through. My dad did the same, generally leaving my mom and me there at the table to finish our meals alone. After one Sunday meal during which neither man had uttered a word, my mom offered a rare observation: "Spoon and your dad are like wounded hawks scanning the rock edge of a cliff, looking for a perch but never quite finding a safe place to land."

△ △ △

After an unseasonably dry fall, winter hit quickly. Back-to-back snowstorms counterpunched the ranch, covering the valley with a two-foot blanket of season-changing snow. Spoon and I spent lots of our evenings in the old bunk-house, mending tack and shooting the breeze. During the day we traveled our winter range on snow machines, dragging food sleighs filled with hay and supplemental cottonseed cake for the cattle.

One evening during early winter when the humidity and temperature had locked in at dead-even thirties, Spoon, seemingly in a reflective mood, told me about a man he'd served with in Vietnam. A friend of his who'd dreamed of returning stateside to become a wildlife illustrator.

"His specialty was drawin' birds," Spoon said as we stood sipping Cokes inside the bunkhouse, each of us leaning against one of the identical ninety-year-old steel-pipe saddle stands my granddad had fabricated and bolted to the floor. "And not just any birds, but what he liked to call diminutives—miniatures to you and me."

Spoon smiled at the chance to be instructive. "The boy could draw anything, from birds to a tropical rain forest fulla bamboo trees. When I asked him one day how long he'd been drawin', just after we came back from patrollin' a three-mile stretch of river, he told me since grade school."

Spoon looked skyward, assessing, calculating, frowning. "Takes time to meet perfection, TJ. Time, perseverance, and a whole lotta patience. My friend Willie Coleman knew that."

I found myself thinking about fly-fishing and the patience and persistence I knew it took to become an expert at the sport. I was good at it, darn good, but nowhere near expert. Reflecting on Spoon's words, I thought about my tendency to be quick on the draw when it came to hooking a fish, especially a lunker, aware that my often-errant quickness had less to do with a lack of technical skill than with mere restraint. "So what ever happened to your friend Coleman?" I asked.

A curtain of sadness spread across Spoon's face. "Got killed one day durin' a search-and-rescue mission. Never had a chance. A twelve-year-old boy with a machine gun came up at him outta the bottom of a sampan we were searchin'."

Spoon stroked his chin thoughtfully. "Always told myself Coleman shoulda been more prepared for the situation, but he wasn't. He wasn't expectin' no twelve-year-old to be a killer. Don't never forget that preparation's as important as patience and persistence when it comes to most things in life, TJ. If a man's gonna survive, he best understand that."

Spoon set his Coke can aside and swatted at a winter-hatch deerfly that had been buzzing him. "Just as important to remember that persistence can be a double-edged sword sometimes—that it can get you into trouble just as quick as not." He rubbed his neck and smiled. "Especially when it comes to women."

I smiled back, wondering what adventures or misadventures Spoon might have had with women. I waited, eager to hear him out, but he went mum all of a sudden, and since I had no intention of telling him about my own failures in that regard, the conversation petered out.

△ △ △

During our first subzero hard winter freeze, Spoon and I spent most of the day tossing cake to hungry cows. We'd just finished running a cottonwood break, and I'd cut my snow machine's engine near the break's open end.

Spoon coasted up next to me, engine off, and scooped up a ball of snow. He packed it lightly with both hands, stood up, and tossed the snowball into the wind. When the snowball broke apart, twisting away on the breeze, Spoon tilted his head back and sniffed the air. "We better get back to headquarters," he said, slipping back down into his seat.

"After a couple more runs," I said.

"Not today. It's gonna dump."

There was a cloud bank to the north, but the sky was otherwise clear. I could even see wisps of smoke rising from the chimneys in the foothills.

"We've got time," I said.

Spoon shrugged and started his machine. "You're the boss."

It took us close to thirty minutes to return to head-quarters, pack up our sleighs with another load of hay and cake, and get back out to the cows. By then a slate gray ceiling of snow clouds hovered over the valley floor. A stiff twenty-miles-an-hour wind had the cattle tightly bunched. We rode along the edge of the huddle drop-ping feed, the noise of our snow machines echoing on the wind. I noticed Spoon continually checking the sky as the smells of gasoline and cottonseed permeated the air. When we dropped the last of our feed, I waved for Spoon to head back for one more load.

"Last run," I hollered, bringing my snow machine to a stop.

Spoon shook his head. "I don't think so," he shouted, pulling even with me. He turned and eyed the cattle.

"We better move these twenty head into the cedar grove and move out quick."

Seconds later the first wet flakes of snow dusted my snow machine's warm engine bonnet, and tears of water streamed down its side. By the time we finished moving the cattle into the trees, snow was coming down in steady sheets, blowing sideways, cutting into our faces like the sharp edge of a knife. Soon ground blizzards kicked up, peppering us with icy pellets of snow, and in no time our eyebrows were frosted cauliflower stubs. The wind became so fierce that we could barely make out the cattle that were less than a stone's throw away, huddled side to side and head to butt in a solid block.

Pressed to do something or likely freeze to death, we ditched our feed sleighs and tied the two snow machines together with a four-foot rope. Spoon pulled me from my machine, hollered, "Get on the back," jumped back on the lead machine, and took off at full throttle. It took us nearly an hour to travel the three miles back to the house, with Spoon skillfully threading his way around treacherous frozen irrigation ditches and eight-foot gully drop-offs all the way. Most of that time he stayed hunkered on his knees, leaning into a thirty-miles-an-hour wind, trying to keep it from blowing us both into an icy open grave. By the time we reached the bunkhouse, we were both plaster casts of ice and snow.

Later, as we thawed out in the cherry glow from the tack room's fully stoked potbellied stove, I watched heat shadows dance around the room. As we tried to stroke some hint of circulation back into our feet, Spoon moved his partially thawed eyebrows up and down out of sync.

"I told you it was gonna dump," he said.

Those were the only words he spoke to me until twenty minutes later, when I got up to leave, he said, "See you in the a.m. 'bout six."

The storm lasted three full days. We lost twenty-five mother cows, a couple of quarter horses, and twenty tons of hay as the valley struggled without power for nearly a week. My dad called it the devil's work and cussed at the sky. In the spring, when we'd feel the money crunch from a shortage of calves, I knew he'd curse the blizzard even more.

△ △ △

Two weeks after the storm, during a fifty-degree mid-January teaser thaw, my mom came home from church and announced to my dad and me that she was certain Spoon had the gift of clairvoyance.

"How else could you explain him knowing in advance about the storm, or that we'd lose exactly two horses, or that our electricity would be out for precisely thirty-three hours?" she asked.

"A blind man could've predicted that snow," grumbled my dad.

My mom looked at him as if she wouldn't have expected him to understand. From then on, whenever she passed out the daily work chits, she'd ask Spoon if he expected bad weather or good.

When spring calving season arrived, our cows had no problem births, thanks in part to Spoon's encouraging efforts, and we never pulled a single cow. I watched Spoon sweet-talk twelve-hundred-pound cattle, slapping them affectionately on the rumps when they refused to move when he wanted them to. Sometimes he even whispered in their ears. His specialty was coaxing cows in labor, pleading with them to deliver while down on his knees, looking at them eye to eye. When I told him he should have been a vet, he said, "How do you know I ain't?"

One blustery March afternoon, we were walking a wind-cleared meadow of stubble hay, double-checking cattle ear tags and brands, when Spoon again seemed to know much more than I could have guessed. Like my mom, I began to believe in his ability to see the future. Federal Land Bank had sent my dad a past-due mortgage notice a couple of days earlier, and since then we'd been busy tallying up the exact number of cattle in our herd. The ground wasn't quite frozen, and our boots left shallow imprints in the grass as we worked.

"Your pa worries too much," said Spoon, who I was certain knew nothing of the bank notice. "Don't conjure up monsters and they won't eat you in your sleep. Tell myself that every day."

"He's doing the best he can," I said, surprised at how quickly I came to my dad's defense.

"Things'll smooth out," said Spoon.

We walked on in silence, weaving between cattle to an open, sunny spot in the middle of the meadow.

"See that cow over there? She's gonna twin," said Spoon, stopping in his tracks to point out a Black Baldy who was scratching her rump on a sagging corner post.

"And the one next to her, the Brock, she'll lose her calf. You any good at graftin' a calf?"

Aware that grafting was a way of fooling a cow into mothering a calf that wasn't her own, I said yes. I hadn't grafted a calf in years because my dad called the process witchcraft—for him, grafting was a time-consuming, bloody mess that never seemed to work. Spoon claimed, however, that the secret to grafting was simply knowing what to do ahead of time and sticking to it.

That night, after the Black Baldy had twins and the Brock delivered a stillborn calf, I watched Spoon drag the stillborn carcass to the calving shed and skin it from one shoulder to under the tail. Using a nail for a needle and baling wire for thread, he sewed the dead calf's skin over one of the Black Baldy twins, then ushered the grafted calf out into the corral. The mother of the stillborn sniffed the grafted calf from head to toe, licking at the awkwardly fitting coat. After a few minutes of indecision, she finally let the calf begin to nurse.

In silence, Spoon walked back into the shed and started cleaning up. He brushed bloody clumps of cedar chips from the floor into a single pile and tossed them into an oil drum by the door. Next he raked fresh cedar chips in to fill the voids. Finally, he covered the floor with a new layer of cedar, threw what remained of the calf carcass into the drum, and walked over to me with a smile. I looked at the spot where he'd worked so feverishly to graft the calf. Footprints were the only evidence of his work.

△ △ △

The next morning my dad and I stood on our front porch sipping coffee and talking. Steam rose from our mugs, evaporating quickly in the dry, crisp morning air.

"Graftin' is a matter of luck," he said, slowly swirling the coffee around in his mug. "Spoon's a gambler who's got a damn good relationship with luck. Remember, I hired him on a bet."

Seconds later Spoon came walking toward us from the tack room in long, measured strides. His boots were caked with mud and a layer of dried blood. He tugged at his work gloves as he approached. He wasn't generally very talkative in the morning, but when he stepped up onto the porch, the look on his face told me he had something important to say.

"Better think about a new way of irrigatin' this spring," he said, looking directly at my dad before scraping a clump of mud off the side of his boot. "We're gonna have trouble with water for sure 'cause your irrigation ditches are way outta balance."

My dad simply stared off into the distance.

Spoon cleared his throat. "Your water ain't balanced," he said, louder than before.

"You read palms too?" asked my dad, suddenly eye to eye with Spoon.

Spoon kicked a cake of dirt from under the heel of his boot. The dirt cartwheeled down the steps. "You're outta balance, and we're in for a drought," he said matter-of-factly.

Dad clenched his teeth and covered his mug, trapping in the rising steam. "I've run water in every ditch on this place for more than thirty-five years, and I've never had a problem. I think I know what I'm doin', Mr. Witherspoon. You can keep your fantasies to yourself."

It was the first time I'd ever heard my dad use Spoon's full last name.

They looked at one another, both ill at ease, for several seconds before my dad tossed his coffee out into the yard, turned, and disappeared into the house. He was back in a flash, waving Spoon's job ticket in his hand. "You're working motor pool the rest of the week, Spoon. Think it's time you leave the ranchin' to me."

Spoon shrugged, stuck the chit in his hatband, rushed down the porch steps, and walked back up the drive.

Three

The problems with our hay meadows started late that spring. The Willow Creek runoff was a ghost of its normal self, and every irrigation ditch on the ranch ran close to creek-bottom dry. Only one ditch in ten had topsoil wet enough to grow a patch of weeds, and the berms along the edges were turning into granular mounds that sometimes blew across the hay meadows like pollen in the wind. Spoon and I rotated the cattle on what little grass we had, hoping to cut down on overgrazing, looking all the while for a runoff we knew would never come. My dad complained that without water it was only a matter of time before the banking bureaucrats fanned out like locusts and began foreclosing on land all along the valley floor.

The last ten days in April, I checked our Willow Creek headgate twice a day, only to realize that by day ten, even without us drawing a single drop at the headgate, the water level had dropped more than a foot. When the first of May rolled around, every rancher in the valley was whispering drought.

Late one evening during that first week of May, I was fly-fishing and getting skunked in a shallow Willow Creek pool normally filled with twenty-inch browns as mayflies rose from the water's surface, drifting off in the dry twilight air. I heard a truck on the access road behind me and turned to watch Spoon bump toward me in one of our pickups with worn-out shocks, squeaking all the way. He pulled to a stop fifty yards short of the stream and shouted, "I've got a remedy," from the cab.

"For what?" I called back.

"For the drought. Come take a look."

I tugged at the suspenders of my hip waders as I walked up the creekbank and across a grassy slope toward the truck. Spoon was already fidgeting with the tailgate chain. The truck bed was filled with eight-inch-diameter PVC drainage pipe.

"If you can't bring Moses to the mountain, you gotta find another way," he said. "We'll pump the damn water down from springs or the Willow Creek headwaters up in the hills."

I laid my rod in the truck bed, shook my head, and eyed the surrounding foothills. "I don't know," I said, unconvinced.

"You'll see," said Spoon, slamming the tailgate. "You'll see."

The next morning, an hour before dawn, Spoon shook me from a hazy twilight sleep.

"What's up?" I asked, blinking back fragmented dreams.

"We need to get started before your pa passes a job ticket my way," Spoon whispered.

"I told you yesterday, we'll just be spitting into the wind. There's not enough water in Willow Creek, even at the source, to douse a campfire."

"Not the way it's set up now, usin' gravity feed to

flood your meadows, but there's plenty of water if we pump it down from the foothills. Come on outside and see what I've got rigged up."

I slipped into a pair of jeans and spread a dab of toothpaste on my thumb. Sucking the paste between my teeth, I inhaled the minty flavor and followed Spoon outside.

Years before, my dad had bought a cable-drum Caterpillar RD6 tracklayer. He'd been using it to backfill around a foundation the day Jimmy had died. The next day he had parked it in the machine shed and covered it with an oily tarp. I stumbled behind Spoon into breaking daylight to see the RD6 idling forty yards down the driveway, a dozer blade on the front. A backhoe arm and bucket swung from the Cat's rear.

"Where'd you get the blade and the bucket?" I asked, astonished.

"Sometimes the Crows beat you. Sometimes you beat the Crows," said Spoon, forcing back a grin. "Hop on; we're goin' for a ride."

The stretch from our hay meadows nearest the house to the headwaters of Willow Creek was a two-mile uphill grade. On the way, dragging a load of PVC pipe behind us in a cart, Spoon told me he was going to build a pump-assisted headwaters diversion levee that would be capable of carrying water to every hay meadow on the ranch.

"You've got first water rights on the creek. I checked 'em out in Hardin," he said.

I knew my dad hadn't looked at our water rights in years, although he'd once carried every bit of water information concerning the place in his head, down to the precise hour we were required to pass our water flow downstream. Once he'd known every ditch rider and water engineer in the state, but times had changed.

"Does my dad know about your plan?" I asked.

"No."

"He'll blow a fuse."

"Not if he don't know," said Spoon. "I figure the levee construction will take us no more than a coupla days, includin' the spring development, the backfill, and settin' the pump. He won't miss us. Besides, it's two miles back down to the house, and he can't hear us, and your mom said she would help."

"You conned her too?"

Spoon looked hurt. "She's just gonna guide your pa's work the opposite direction from ours. We'll be done before he knows a thing."

"He'll can you when he finds out."

"I don't think so, but if he does, won't be nothin' new."

"What if he looks for the Cat?"

"I threw the tarp back over sixty bales of hay. Shaped 'em up to look like the Cat. I just hope he don't hear us grindin' our way up this hill," said Spoon, easing the RD6 into a lower gear.

The backhoe bucket swung back and forth in a U until we were on a level spot a third of the way up Willow Creek grade. When we crossed the creek only a few yards from where Jimmy had drowned, I felt a lump in my throat, maybe even a little bitterness. In a sense, it was Jimmy who was shielding us from detection.

During irrigation season my dad had me handle all the high-country ditches; because of Jimmy, he rarely ventured up the grade.

I watched the creek's low, clear water thread its way around a couple of boulders before knifing into an undercut along the bank and thought how, at that moment, Jimmy could have walked across the stream.

"We won't have to worry too much about my dad coming up here," I said.

Spoon didn't respond until several moments later. He seemed to know exactly what I was thinking. "If you don't face up to the shadows in your life, sooner or later they'll block out all the light."

During a normal spring runoff, the Willow Creek headwaters thundered unrestrained down the steep grade to the valley floor below. That day, we were greeted by the peaceful sound of a meandering brook. There hadn't been snowpack in the mountains for over two months, and the water table was at a sixty-year low. Spoon pulled the Cat to a stop, then turned it around in a slow half circle until the blade pointed back down the hill. A thicket of greening willows followed the creekbed in a lazy S before folding out into the meadow below.

"We're gonna run a four-foot-wide ditch all the way back down," he said, shading his eyes and gazing down at the ranch below. Smiling as if he knew something I didn't, he tossed a six-foot length of PVC pipe at my feet.

We started back down the hill, staking out our levee, setting wooden stakes every thirty feet. By the time we hit the meadow below, a dull ache followed the curvature of my spine. It was close to noon when Spoon, looking agitated, said we needed to get back up top. We started back up the hillside, counting our stakes as we went.

Halfway back, Spoon said, "I've got a Crow comin' to dig a shallow well and help us set a pump."

At the top of the grade a tall, rail-thin Indian was standing near the Cat. He'd driven a pickup in from the backside of our ranch, I later found out, trespassing his way across a neighbor's land. His skin was scarred from acne, and he didn't show any sign of recognition until Spoon was within a couple of feet of him.

"The pipe's in the cart," said Spoon, looking the man square in the eye.

A contraption for shallow-well drilling sat bolted cockeyed to the bed of the Indian's pickup, looking as though it might topple any second.

"Pull your rig over here," said Spoon, pointing to a level spot near the headwaters.

The man hesitated and shook his head. "Too dangerous."

"Don't run chicken on me," said Spoon. "You won't need to move it more'n twenty feet. And you owe me, or have you forgot?"

"Then we're even?" the man asked.

"Even as you ever get in life," said Spoon.

The man pulled his rig over to the spot Spoon had pointed out, and after a few minutes of leveling, cranking, and adjusting his drill, he started a hole. He hit water at about twenty feet, but Spoon made him drill to forty. He then drove casings into the hole, set the pump, and was done an hour later. When he started to permanently cap the well, Spoon walked over.

"No need for that," said Spoon. They said something to one another in a whisper. The man gave Spoon a nod, got back into his rig, and headed down the backside of Willow Creek grade.

Minutes later, Spoon started back down the front of the hillside, following our stakes and cutting a right-of-way with the Cat's blade. I walked along in the track, inhaling the scent of diesel fuel and sage, squaring things up with a shovel. Spoon ran the Cat in low, carving a four-foot-wide path between our stakes all the way down the hill to the open eight-hundred-acre meadow below, never taking out a single stake. A narrow hillside scar was left in the Caterpillar's wake. He turned the Cat on a dime and started back up, digging a trench with the backhoe at the Cat's other end. I followed with the shovel, leveling, squaring, and smoothing the overspill. We stopped close to sundown about halfway up the grade. Spoon assured me that we could finish our irrigation trench, hook up the PVC pipe, and run our test water the next day. A fine mist had settled over the valley as we began our slow walk home. All the way there I couldn't help but wonder and worry about whether my dad had any inkling of what we'd been up to.

△ △ △

The next morning we started at dawn. Dew covered the faded yellow Cat, and it shimmered in the sun.

"We'll finish today," said Spoon, glancing skyward. He hopped up into the Cat's cracked leather seat and started the engine.

We trenched our way back up the grade through a stand of rough timber into a warm-spring glade, and finally back to the mouth of Willow Creek. Hours later Spoon scooped out his last bucket of earth in the warm afternoon sun as I padded up a final berm of dirt around the water source, rounding off the edge. My back muscles felt as tight as case-hardened steel, but when I straightened up, rubbing my side, and looked back down the grade, following the levee until it disappeared into the hay meadow below, all I could do was smile.

"Nothin' to do now but hook 'er up," said Spoon.

I watched Spoon jerry-rig a generator and battery system to run off the engine of the RD6. He mounted the whole thing with floodlights, explaining that with a little diesel fuel, his makeshift generator could run twenty-four hours a day. "There's plenty of water up here. Enough to guarantee we'll get two cuttin's of hay. Plenty for feed—plenty to sell," he said with a grin.

An hour before sunset we sent our first trickle of water downhill. Fifteen minutes later there was a steady stream.

"Better any day than some temperamental damn creek," said Spoon, slapping the side of the Cat. "We've tapped the source."

"No question," I answered, watching the water roll.

"Next we'll ditch out the south pasture, then the west-end flats," said Spoon, breaking into a quick, satisfied grin.

But then as suddenly as the grin had appeared, it was gone. "Ain't quite figured out how to break it to your pa yet, though. I might need a little help with that."

"What can he say?"

"Things neither of us wanna hear," said Spoon. "Especially since we're usin' his old Cat for a generator."

We started our walk back down the hill, Spoon carrying a shovel, I dragging a rake. Thin, wispy clouds drifted by, looking like campfire smoke rising in the evening air. As we walked, the lone spur on Spoon's right boot jingled out a lopsided cadence.

◁ ◁ ◁

I didn't see the horse and rider until I heard the sound of hoofbeats twenty yards away. My dad brought his horse, Smokey, to a halt a few feet from the irrigation trench as Spoon and I continued walking his way.

Very deliberately, dad dismounted, and once he was on the ground Smokey took a long, slow drink from the new ditch. In the level glade the ditch ran more slowly than at the top, and the water seemed to simply meander by.

"Somebody went to a hell of a lot of work to run this trench," my dad said, eyeing Spoon pensively before locking his gaze on me.

I forced a smile, hoping it would ease what I suspected was coming, but it failed to break his cold, hard stare.

"You two should've put more effort into makin' sure I wouldn't know what you were up to," he said, staring at the water as if he expected it to stop.

"I had to drag TJ kickin' and screamin' all the way," Spoon said, coming to my defense.

My dad paced back and forth along the trench in broad, measured steps. He was clearly nervous, walking ground he hadn't walked, much less seen, in years. He looked around the clearing, scanning it slowly as if he somehow thought he needed permission to be there.

"What if the sky opens up and we break this drought?" he asked. "What good is a penny-ante unpermitted levee to us then?"

Spoon answered quickly. Once again he seemed to know the question before it had been asked. "We can cut back the pump from its current flow of five hundred gallons a minute to as low as fifty if need be, but we're in for a low-water mark around here for three, maybe even four years."

"You're sure of that?" asked my dad, challenging Spoon with his eyes.

"As sure as my name's Arcus Witherspoon."

Deep in thought, my dad walked over to a stand of quaking aspen, then back to the spot where Jimmy had drowned. The tree closest to him was thirty feet high. Elk had antler-notched the trunk just above my dad's head. He picked at the trunk, snapping off a piece of bark. His eyes looked sad and uncertain. "These trees were no more than saplings twenty years ago," he said with a sigh. "Seems like you can't hold back somethin' when it decides it wants to grow. Come over here and I'll show you somethin'," he said, motioning for us to follow.

We crossed a dry creekbed and walked over to a small island between our new irrigation ditch and Willow Creek.

In the middle of the island, a half-ton boulder jutted out at us.

"This boulder must sink down pretty deep," said my dad. "Time was, it was mostly covered by water, sittin' in the middle of the creek. Now it's out here by itself. Guess it'll never move."

"It might not be stuck down as deep as you think," Spoon said.

Looking at my dad, ashen and trembling, it seemed like he was staring directly down a pipeline to the past.

Dad stared at the boulder for a while, then put his shoulder to it, trying to move it by himself. When the boulder didn't budge, Spoon and I offered a hand. The three of us struggled with the rock for what seemed like an eternity until finally a circle of dirt broke around the base, and we all stepped back, out of breath.

"We can try it with the Cat," said Spoon.

"No," said my dad. "All it needed was a little loosening up. Movin' it can wait."

Dad walked over to Smokey and gathered up the reins. "Did I ever tell you about my dad's cattle empire?" he asked Spoon, looking as if he'd suddenly just shed a lifelong burden.

"Nope," Spoon replied.

"Well, maybe I'll fill you in when we get back to the house."

We started walking down the hillside three abreast. After a while my dad handed me Smokey's reins. I felt the big, sometimes stubborn gelding plodding along easily behind me, warm breath from his nostrils pushing us ahead.

△ △ △

We left that boulder there, and to this day it stands as a landmark or a headstone. Probably a little of both. My dad later brought the Cat back down the hill, and nothing more was ever said between the three of us about the levee. The incident inched us all a bit closer, but not so close that my dad and Spoon were on the same page. They'd simply made it to being in the same book.

△ △ △

Working side by side, and sweating through an unexpected late-spring spell of heat over the next two weeks, we finished up the irrigation project. My dad cursed every rock and gopher hole as we worked while Spoon, ever on the lookout for rattlesnakes, killed more than his share. I enjoyed the uneasy peace between the two of them as we worked, but deep down I knew it was a peace that couldn't last.

Four

A few days after wrapping up the levee project, Spoon, my dad, and I were setting a couple of brace posts at the southeast corner of one of our meadows, a meadow that had never produced the kind of hay it should have. Suddenly Spoon, who'd been acting a bit out of sorts all day, constantly looking over his shoulder as if something or someone might be gaining on him, looked up from his posthole tamper, eyed the ice blue sky, inhaled deeply, and said, more to himself than to me or my dad, "There's trouble brewin'. I can smell it."

Ever skeptical of Spoon's odd pronouncements, even in the face of our levee success, my dad asked, "You worried we've got a new den of sidewinders we're gonna have to contend with?"

Sounding somber and reflective, Spoon simply said, "I wish."

Dad responded with a grunt and went back to wrestling the stubborn brace post. But Spoon's pronouncement stuck with me the rest of the day, and the day after that—and I had a feeling that it had also resonated with my dad, even though he hadn't shown it.

◁ ◁ ◁

Driving along one of our south pasture irrigation ditches with Spoon a couple of days after his declaration of trouble and feeling amazingly self-satisfied, I watched water gurgle its way over rock and soil that had been bone dry for years. As we rolled slowly along in one of our vintage, never-say-die John Deere 3020 tractors, checking out the two-mile-long stretch of ditch for seeps and leaks, I had the feeling, in spite of Spoon's prediction of trouble on the horizon, that ranch operations had reached a steady, manageable state.

That feeling of comfort disappeared when Spoon, looking skyward toward a bank of low-hanging clouds, announced in the same ominous tone he'd used the day we set the brace posts, "Things around here ain't gonna stay all cotton fluffy like them clouds up there forever."

Spoon hadn't been in much of a clairvoyant mood—or, for that matter, much of a fraternizing mood—for over a week. He'd been to town for a couple of pieces of cowhide to repair an old, beat-up saddle, but in some sense he didn't seem as usual. He'd been spending most of his free time in his quarters reading books, studying maps, and poring over county records he'd gotten from the county clerk's office or checked out of the Hardin library. Once when I caught him with his nose in a pile of genealogy documents he told me that he had the feeling he was close to zeroing in on his roots once and for all.

"Didn't realize you were in future-seeing mode today," I said, watching the irrigation water work its way across an eighty-acre meadow of thirsty timothy and clover.

"Never really slip outta that mode, TJ. It's just that things gotta have proper reflection."

"So what are you seeing, specifically, about things here at the ranch, for instance?"

With a wink and a troubled smile, he said, "We're all, every one of us here on the place, gonna get tested real soon. I've seen it kinda fuzzylike and jumbled in my head day and night for near a week. When I'm workin' and when I'm dreamin' the vision keeps comin' back. Problem is, I can't quite piece it all together as a yet. All I know is that our will's gonna be tried. Yours and your folks for the most part, but I'll be tested too." He eyed the water in the ditch as if it were somehow a mirror to the future and nodded to himself.

"You sure?"

"As sure as I am that them puffy white clouds sittin' overhead got themselves a bunch of dark distant cousins who'll bring us buckets fulla rain. As sure as I am that a busted-up old bronc-ridin' Crow from Hardin 'name a Saddlefoot who told me the other night I was part Arapahoe and not Cheyenne, like I'd always thought, is likely dead-center right about my heritage. And as sure as I am that I'm gonna have to look at new ways of tracin' out my roots from here on out."

Spoon's tone let me know he was unhappy about wasting precious time following what had turned out to be a dead end.

"So when's the rain coming?" I asked, aware that the forecast had called for clear skies all week.

"By this evenin', TJ. By this evenin' for sure. But for now we got sunshine and work to do, so let's get at it."

"Might as well," I said, giving the old 3020 some gas and searching the sky for nonexistent signs of rain.

△ △ △

Edward Koffman, known around Big Horn County as Easy Ed, was anything but what you'd call easy. He was a fidgety, rotund, always-on-edge squat of a man who seemed to constantly be looking over his shoulder as if for instruction. Koffman arrived at our house just after supper on the evening of Spoon's prediction of rain, during the final stages of a violent thunderstorm that rattled the rafters and, as we discovered later, unhinged a twenty-by-twenty-foot section of metal roof.

Spoon, who very rarely ate with us, had joined us for supper at the insistence of my mom, who'd made her Big Horn County Fair–winning pot roast, roasted corn right off the cob, green beans, corn bread, and fresh apple pie.

Spoon and I were devouring second helpings of pie when my dad got up from his chair to answer the frantic knocking at the front door. He strode across the dining room, coffee mug in hand, mumbling, "Who on earth can that be?" and returned with Koffman in tow.

The russet-skinned, nearly eyebrowless Koffman was a man I knew well. Years earlier he'd tried to get me to befriend his son, a frail, sickly shell of a boy named Henry, with wide gaps between his teeth and the suffocated look of an asthmatic. I'd tried my best to forge a friendship with Henry—played basketball with him, called him Hank, as he'd insisted, spent time trying to teach him how to fly-fish. I'd even tried to teach him to run a tractor and baler, but his mind had always seemed to be elsewhere, lost in some fantasy-filled dream. When he'd died of leukemia several months after my final attempt at fly-fishing instruction, I'd had the sense that perhaps, like Spoon, he'd been able to see his own future.

For months after Henry's death, Koffman had tried to use the fact that he and my dad had both lost sons to wheedle his way into the fabric of our family. But my folks, insightful and circumspect, understood the real reason for Koffman's telephone calls, ambushes while they were in Hardin picking up supplies, and unannounced visits to the ranch. Regardless of his loss, and despite his clumsy attempts to mask his real reasons for trying to ingratiate himself with us, Easy Ed Koffman was a land-grabbing energy company scout, a coal, oil, and gas man of the rankest order. A man who some people in our valley claimed had cheated uninformed and unwitting ranchers out of their mineral rights and occasionally even their land. He'd snookered them not with a six-gun and the intimidating Old West skills of a land-grabbing bully, but with his well-honed New West skills as a corporate lawyer.

Normally calm and collected, my dad looked unhinged by Koffman's intrusion. He sternly eyed my mom, who rose and flashed Koffman her best disingenuous chorus-line dancer's smile. It was a smile she typically reserved for the busybody social-climbing church women whom she detested.

Aware that trouble might well be on the wing, I glanced at Spoon. The look on his face as much as said, *Told you so.*

Everyone remained silent until my mom said graciously, "Afraid you missed supper, Edward. But you're welcome to have dessert with us. Have a seat."

Koffman eyed what was left of the deep-dish pie on the table and sat down. "A man would be a fool to turn down an offer like that, and from the best pastry maker in the county."

"Back-to-back county fair ribbons to prove it," my dad said proudly, glancing at me and shaking his head as Koffman adjusted himself in his chair. "You know TJ, of course, but I don't believe you've met Arcus Witherspoon, my hired man."

"Nope." Koffman stretched across the table, clasped Spoon's hand, and shook it. "Mr. Witherspoon."

Quickly slipping his hand out of Koffman's, Spoon nodded and said, "Just Spoon."

"Just Spoon it is, then. Pleasure."

Koffman eased back in his chair as my mom slid the pie toward her to cut him a slice. "Big, small, or otherwise?" she asked.

"Small." Koffman patted his more-than-ample belly. "Been trying my darnedest to cut back."

"You can start again tomorrow," she said, handing him a plate with a generous slice. "Coffee?"

"No. Don't want to ruin the taste of the pie."

As I watched the man who was the legal front for Acota Energy Corporation devour his dessert, I thought about Henry and wondered whether the boy who'd wanted to be called Hank had ever understood what his dad did for a living. Koffman and Acota were after energy, but, surprisingly, they weren't after our ranch's minuscule amounts of oil, its gas, or even its relatively plentiful shale.

For Acota, those things were small potatoes. What they were after, as everyone at the table but Spoon knew all too well, was the chance to extract the ranch's thousands of acres of coal. Ours was one of the few remaining large-parcel ranches in the valley whose landowner also owned the bulk of the mineral rights. I'd seen documents and maps that my dad kept in a safe-deposit box at the First Interstate Bank of Hardin attesting to the fact. The documents, signed decades earlier by President Warren G. Harding, gave us ownership to what some considered to be the equivalent of gold in an energy-rich state like Montana. Although the government owned the rights to lesser coal deposits surrounding us for untold square miles on Bureau of Land Management land, we, like a handful of other ranchers in the Willow Creek valley, could not only dictate what happened to our own coal reserves, but to some extent controlled access to the politically significant BLM lands.

The largest coal-rich private lands highlighted in green on my dad's sequestered maps included six thousand acres of our ranch and five thousand acres of Willard Johnson's Flying Diamond spread immediately north of us. Johnson, a hot-tempered, no-nonsense, sixty-one-year-old confirmed bachelor who'd had irrigation battles with everyone in the valley, had as little use for Easy Ed Koffman as we did. The ranch adjacent to Johnson's to the south, which abutted both our ranch and the Flying Diamond at one corner, belonged to Beatrice and Rulon Demaster, a land-speculating husband-and-wife team out of New Jersey. When they'd purchased the nine thousand acres five years earlier, the Demasters, at least according to my mom, had no idea that it would be their coal rights that would potentially float their speculative financial boat to its high-water mark, not their oil and gas rights. All three ranches and a fourth, smaller ranch owned by Dale Turpin came together much like the states of Colorado, New Mexico, Utah, and Arizona at a place we called Four Corners.

Finished with his pie, Koffman mashed the remaining crust fragments onto the bottom of his fork and licked the assembled crumbs. Turning his attention to me and smiling, he said, "So what are you gonna do with yourself now that you're out of school, TJ? Smart young man like you, salutatorian of your high school class, college has to be in the future somewhere."

"I guess," I said with a shrug. "But I figured I'd take a year or so off and help out here at the ranch."

"Reasonable." Koffman said, stroking his chin. "Just don't get yourself imprisoned by the sirens of this land. They have beautiful voices that can be awfully enticing. Could be they might entice you to stay forever."

"Something wrong with that?" my dad asked pointedly.

"No, no. Nothing at all," Koffman said, very obviously backpedaling. "But a man needs to keep his options open where it concerns the future, wouldn't you say, TJ?"

"What TJ does with his life will be his doing." There was a note of obvious irritation in my dad's response, one that as much as said, *Butt out, fat boy.* Glancing across the table at me, he said, "Barrister or bronc buster, scientist or farrier, his future's up to him." He shot me a supportive wink. "And right at this moment, notwithstanding the boy's future, he and Spoon have half a dozen horses to corral up and grain."

The authoritative look he flashed let the two of us know that our time at the supper table was over. As we rose from our seats, I glanced at my mom, hoping she'd offer an excuse for us to stay, but the expression on her face, tense and expectant, told me that the conversation was likely to turn in an unpleasant direction.

I was almost to the back door with Spoon close on my heels when my dad called out, "Check Smokey's right hind leg for me, Spoon. He was favorin' it again today." Glancing back at Koffman rather than my dad and with his head cocked, cobralike, Spoon nodded and followed me out the door.

As we walked through a misty drizzle, down a boggy strip of land that earlier in the day had been crusted hard, to round up the horses, Spoon said, "I told you a change was comin'."

"Koffman or the weather?" I asked smugly.

"You know which one," Spoon said, sounding annoyed.

"My dad's handled Koffman before," I said, aware that he'd sent Koffman packing on more than one occasion.

"Yeah, but this time there's a chink in your Willow Creek valley armor."

Spoon stopped short, right in the middle of a mud puddle. I stood there with him as water seeped into my boots, looking skyward through the mist. Stroking one sideburn as if to coalesce his thoughts, Spoon said, "And what's worse than that nick in your breastplate is the fact that Koffman's gonna be bringin' in reinforcements."

I didn't fully understand Spoon's reference to the chink in our Willow Creek armor, nor did I appreciate what he was getting at with his talk about reinforcements. What I did understand, suddenly shivering, with ice water knifing its way between my toes, was that Spoon had been dead on about the rain.

Five

I'm not quite sure why my folks and Koffman didn't get to the meat of their discussion until after I returned from helping Spoon corral the horses to eavesdrop on their conversation from our mudroom. It may have been because Koffman, as my dad was fond of saying, liked to coil a little, rattlesnake-like, before striking. Or maybe he'd opted for another slice of pie while my mom cleared the dishes. Whatever the case, the mudroom turned out to be a perfect box seat for listening.

The room sat catty-corner from the dining room, protected from view by a three-foot-deep archway. It had once been Jimmy's bedroom, and the doorway still had notches in it documenting his height from ages five to fifteen. I sat at the east end of the archway, feeling guilty as I listened in on an echoey conversation that carried along the Spanish-tile floors right through the open mudroom door.

The clink of glassware and china and the smell of cigar smoke, Koffman's for certain, rattled me. I imagined the burly oil, gas, and coal man toying with his cigar, preparing to torture my parents. When words were finally spoken, they were Koffman's.

"Things like that get exaggerated, Marva," he said. "It's common around these parts. I never told Willard Johnson that the Demasters had signed anything related to the lease of their coal rights, or that by holding out he'd lose the same good price. Nor did I switch stories for the Demasters. Let's just say that I provided the two parties with the incentive they needed to make a choice. To in fact do what they were already inclined to do. The Demasters made the prudent choice. As for Johnson, he'll come around."

"And by inference, I'm guessin' you think we will as well," my dad said.

There was no immediate answer. I could almost feel Koffman taking a long drag on his cigar and smiling slyly. The discussion took a sharp turn when he finally spoke.

"Listen a little more carefully, Bill. Be a bit more objective, and you'll see that my offer makes sound economic and, from your point of view, environmental sense. You've got top-grade, low-sulfur coal beneath the overburden of dirt you're so intent on running a dying cattle empire on. The kind of coal that doesn't choke the environment. You have a chance to make a defining sensible statement, one that says, 'I care about the land,' and that can also be quite profitable. I showed you the figures last spring. It's been almost a year. We need some movement here. You know as well as I do that only a small portion of your land can be mined. No more than a tenth of the entire fourteen thousand acres. But that tenth contains a considerable amount of coal." Koffman paused as if to allow his words to gather steam. "While we're mining and increasing your bank account, you of course can keep on ranching."

My eyes widened, and I flinched as Koffman cleared his throat. I had the urge to charge into the dining room and shove his cigar down that throat, but having been taught that patience generally trumps haste and intolerance, I adjusted my weight onto my right knee, leaned against the wall, slapped a damper on my anger, and continued listening.

"I've been told that no matter how beautiful or ripe the land out here appears from a distance in any given year, it nonetheless takes thirty to thirty-five acres of grass to fatten a calf," said Koffman. "That's a lot of land per animal. You could do a whole lot better. My geologists tell me that you and your missus own land with a seam of coal that can easily earn you royalties in the neighborhood of a hundred eighty thousand dollars every twenty-four months. More than you make on any amount of beef you run, I'd wager."

My dad's response started as a low rumble that slowly rose to a higher, aggravated pitch. "You're slick, Koffman. Slick as rain-drenched claystone. Although you were a mite too obvious earlier, aimin' your words at Marva rather than me. Could be that on your ride out here you came to the conclusion that she might be a little easier to sell, but you're wrong. We're a solid block of granite, me, her, and TJ. You're wrong about us makin' a living at running cattle. Wrong thinkin' we have your thirst for money and wrong about what would happen to that fourteen hundred acres of our land you'd end up mining. My guess is that Acota's a very hungry beast. Hungry for more than a mere tenth of fourteen thousand acres. You'd start off small, all right, but the beast's appetite would increase, and soon you'd want a twenty-acre staging area for your loaders and graders. Next, ten or fifteen more for your trucks and your cuttin' machines. And then another fifty for a gasification plant when you figured out there was oil under the land as well. Eventually you'd expand your operations to include a pig-ugly two- or three-hundred-acre trailer town.

"Believe me, I know the drill. In the end you'd hope to wear us down, thinkin' we'd eventually figure it would be easier to go along to get along. Easier still to ignore the eyesore you were creating. You'd bet on the fact that I'd come over to your way of thinkin' because I'd get so exasperated and in love with money. That in the end I'd give up a quarter of the ranch and then another quarter until our solitude and sense of place were lost and we retreated somewhere else, away from a place of beauty that no longer looked or even smelled like it did at the start. I'd bet a prize bull that briefcase you carried in contains a new version of the contract you waved at me last spring. But whether it does or not, you'll never get the chance to strip-mine my land. Not now, not ever!"

Koffman suppressed a cough. "You're a hard sell, Bill. As tough a nut as I've ever run into. Have you ever considered the fact that our country and our way of life demand coal? We've got an energy problem on our hands here in the U-S-of-A, in case you've missed it. One that's not going away anytime soon."

This time it was my mom who responded. "Put away your flag, Mr. Koffman. You're talking to a Korean War veteran, in case you didn't know it. One who earned not one, but a couple of Purple Hearts."

"So I am. And my company and I appreciate your service. But what about your son? Where does he fit in all this?"

The hairs on the back of my neck bristled. Gritting my teeth and thinking, *You arrogant, condescending asshole,* I cupped my hand to my ear, determined not to miss a single word.

"More importantly," Koffman challenged, "what about your legacy and your responsibility—no, your *obligation* to your son?"

My mom's gasp failed to stop Koffman.

"As you well know, we at Acota are in this for the long haul, and in the long run, governments, fortunately for us and perhaps unfortunately for you, usually side with the interests of energy. So your decision, although you may see it as an independent or perhaps even a misguided libertarian one, will ultimately be of consequence to your son. It could be that he would prefer security to ranching."

"And that would be his choice," my dad shot back. "Always will be. Unlike my cattle herd, I don't own TJ."

"Then perhaps I should have a talk with him. Don't you think he's old enough to have earned a say in this?"

"Don't you dare!" my mom said. Her words came out one by one, harsh and steely.

I rose to a sprinter's squat, prepared to race into the dining room and knock Koffman out of his chair. But before I could, my dad said in a calm but authoritative voice, the kind of voice that carried a sledgehammer of meaning in every word, "Bother TJ and we'll tangle, Koffman. Tangle in the ugly, primitive, animalistic sense of the word. There'll be no politeness, just a battle. One I guarantee you won't win."

"You sound very certain of yourself."

"As certain as I am that escortin' you to the door and telling you to never set foot on my doorstep again will, in a most civilized way, serve to bring total severance to these discussions. There'll be no more polite cat-and-mouse talk around a dinner table if you return. I don't know about you, but I've been to war. It's a place that no one but a fool wants to be, but I'll go there again, and gladly, if you press the issue or ever have the nerve to try to talk to TJ."

The shuffle of feet and the sound of chairs sliding across the dining room hardwood told me that the conversation was over.

"So you say," Koffman said with an air of certainty that sent a chill down my spine. "But in the end, someone named Darley will talk with me. It's the way of the world."

"You may leave now, Mr. Koffman," my mom said pointedly.

Within seconds I heard the heavy clump of booted footsteps moving across the dining room toward the front door. When the front door creaked open and then slammed, I hoped that Easy Ed Koffman was gone from our lives forever. My dad's easily discernible long, heavy-hitting strides had him back in the dining room quickly.

"Guess we're sticking," said my mom.

"Until they scrape us off with the buffalo grass, sweet clover, and sage," my dad said defiantly.

"I don't like Koffman, Bill. There's something not just disingenuous, but darkly clever and calculating about him.

And the way he lit up that cigar without asking permission—
he's unbelievably arrogant as well."

"You'll get no argument from me, but those aren't
the things that worry me."

"Then what does? That he'll talk to TJ?"

"No. TJ's you and me put together, and in a lot of
ways he's a harder rock than either of us."

"Then what?"

Dad's voice trailed off to a whisper. "Koffman's the
tip of an iceberg, Marva. The sharp point of a knife that
Acota would like to bury in us to the hilt. What I'm worried about is that, like the North Koreans at Chosen and
the Vietcong at Tet, Koffman's got an army of reinforcements waitin' in the wings."

I knew my dad's words could only serve to upset my
mom. They always did when he mentioned Korea or the
war her youngest brother had been killed in, Vietnam.
His assessment, however, had me thinking about what
Spoon had said about our family being tested. I felt decid-
edly unsteady as I stood.

"Do you think it'll get messy, Bill?" Mom asked.

I pictured dad smiling and draping his arm reassuringly over her shoulder as he answered, "Not really, Marva.
Not really."

But I knew as I retreated silently from the mudroom
and stepped out into the backyard to head for Spoon's
quarters that, all reassurances aside, we were in for a battle. Uncertain whether to tell Spoon all of what I'd overheard, I paused in the darkness to collect my thoughts.

As I crossed Koffman's fresh bootprints in the soil, I

had the strange sense that Spoon already knew what had happened and that his lights were on simply to let me know that he'd been patiently waiting.

Six

I don't know how on earth Spoon knew I was about to knock on his door. I couldn't be sure whether he'd heard me tiptoe up to the tack room, watched my approach from a window, or simply felt my presence, but as I prepared to knock, the door swung open, and Spoon, standing barefoot in the doorway, wearing a sleeveless T-shirt and faded jeans that looked as if they'd been washed a thousand times, smiled and said, "Come on in."

I'd never really paid attention to how muscular his upper body was, but for some reason he looked less coiled and wiry than usual, and a lot more physically powerful.

"What's got you scurryin' around here this time of night?" he asked, waving me in.

Shaking my head, I said, "A problem."

"Can't be all that bad. You're still upright." His coarse, jet-black, nearly shoulder-length hair moved as if the wind was in it as we walked across the once-disordered room that was now as neat as a pin and Spoon's home. I eyed the antelope head mounted on the wall above the room's potbellied stove. Jimmy had shot the five-point buck late one fall. Dad had had the head stuffed and mounted in Billings, but after Jimmy's death he'd tossed the trophy into a corner of our machine shop, where it had remained for years among coffee cans full of nuts and bolts and discarded shop rags. Spoon had discovered it one spring day. Recognizing something special about the neglected old buck, he'd spent hours cleaning it and combing it out, eventually bringing it back to its original lifelike, taxidermic state.

"You and old Malcolm there seem to be communicatin'." Spoon reached up, patted the antelope head, smiled, and took a seat. "Could be you knew each other in another life. Now, tell me about your problem."

"It's not my problem, really. It's actually a problem for my folks."

"Any problem of theirs is ultimately gonna be yours, TJ. You're savvy enough to know that."

"Guess so."

"Guessin's for stockbrokers and politicians, son, not for us cattle-ranchin' types. When you're facin' a real problem, it's best to steer clear of guesswork."

"I didn't say the problem had to do with the ranch."

"You didn't have to." Spoon sucked a stream of air through the gap between his top two front teeth. "I saw your problem when he arrived. All blustery and wind driven, and in a rainstorm to make matters worse. Who was he?"

"Name's Koffman. He's a bigwig at Acota Energy. The oil and gas folks."

"And coal," Spoon said insightfully. "So what was his mission out here?"

"He wants our coal."

"And people in hell want ice water," Spoon said with a smile.

"It's not funny, Spoon. Koffman hinted to my folks

that he got the Demasters to sign off on leasing their coal rights to Acota. I think he was probably telling the truth."

"He'll need to lease more property than that to make any kinda minin' proposition pencil out for a big company like Acota. Trust me."

Pondering how Spoon could possibly know how much leased land Acota needed to run its operations in the black, I said, "He's batting .333. He's got one ranch out of the big three in this valley. In baseball terms, he'd be considered a slugger."

Spoon frowned, and a rock-solid serious look crossed his face. "But this ain't a baseball game, TJ. Out here in the real world, it's generally all or none. You're right about one thing, though. Koffman's got his foot in the door, and that's a problem."

Then, without asking me how I knew so much about the discussion between Koffman and my parents, Spoon stroked his chin thoughtfully and said, "I'm guessin' that right now Koffman's only scratchin' at the dirt, lookin' for a way to unearth a bone. That's the good part. The bad part, unfortunately, is that he'll keep on diggin'."

"If Koffman and his Acota people come in here, they'll turn the place into a zoo," I said angrily. "It'll stink like a power plant, and everybody knows the grazing will never be the same, regardless of what Acota says about reclaiming the land."

Nodding in agreement, Spoon said, "Then we won't let 'em."

Thrilled at Spoon's response but concerned that he didn't fully appreciate the gravity of the situation, I said,

"Dad ended up mentioning Korea to Koffman before he ushered him out of the house. You know he'd never do that, especially in front of my mom, unless he was truly upset." I was well aware that Spoon and my dad had occasionally shared their combat experiences with each other, but the surprised look on Spoon's face told me he hadn't realized that I had paid any attention to those chats.

"I see." Spoon drummed his fingers on the overstuffed leather chair he'd salvaged from a flea market and restored. He seemed to be storing up what I'd just told him for discussion at a later date. Looking up at Malcolm as if he expected the old five-point buck to offer a bolt of wisdom, he said, "So what we've got when it all shakes out is an energy company hungry for the coal underneath your land, and your pa soundin' like he's preparin' to go into battle. How'd your ma respond durin' the talk with Koffman?"

"I think she would've tossed him out of the house on his ear if she'd had her way."

Spoon, who'd been partial to my mom since the first day he'd set foot on the ranch, said, "Tells me all I need to know right there."

"There is one other thing," I said tentatively. "Koffman talked as if he planned to use me as a bargaining chip. Claimed I had a right to the decision making when it came to the ranch."

"He's a smart one," said Spoon, shaking his head. "Devil's kin generally are. Sounds like he knows how to separate blood from money. You got any idea what the annual royalties would be on the coal Acota could dig up off this place?"

"Not really, although Koffman mentioned hundreds of thousands."

"I'd say he's on the light side," said Spoon. "If he could get you and your folks wranglin' over the potential earnings, he'd have a fightin' chance of winnin' his little game. Maybe not right now, but somewhere down the line. Especially if you go off to college, earn yourself a couple of low-profit-margin degrees, and decide this land here's a better investment than your education."

"No way in hell!"

"I know that, TJ. But like it or not, the life that's out there waitin' for you really don't. Like they say, shit happens. Sickness, agin' parents, a wife, a family, kids."

I flashed Spoon as defiant a look as I could muster and shook my head. "I'd sooner die than lose one acre of this land."

I was as stitched to the land as my dad. I'd walked, driven, or ridden every acre of our place on horseback. I'd seen it blanketed by snows and parched in drought. I'd brought some of my townie classmates from Hardin out to Willow Creek for show-and-tell as a third-grader, proudly showed them several fence posts I'd helped my dad set, and, with the aid of a ladder for access, even started one of our tractors for them. Willow Creek was as much a part of me as my skin. I couldn't imagine giving up a single clump of earth on the place to anyone, especially Koffman.

"I expect you would. And I expect Mr. Koffman probably knows that too. Knows and understands that you, your ma, and your pa are a solid brick wall he'll need to knock down. That's why you can bet he ain't in this all by his lonesome. You got folks who support you—so does he." Spoon eyed the hundred-year-old three-gray-hills Navajo rug that covered much of the room's wide-plank flooring. "Count on it."

I found myself thinking, as we both stared at the rug that had been destined for the scrap heap before Spoon's arrival, how it always came down to Spoon knowing things. He'd known the value of the rug the instant he'd seen it, although to my knowledge he was neither a rug merchant nor a collector. He'd unrolled the rug in front of my mom one evening a few weeks after his arrival and suggested to her that it was valuable enough to warrant an appraisal. After a week of prodding, she'd convinced my dad to take her to Billings and have it appraised. I'd tagged along. When the appraisal had come in at eighteen thousand dollars, it had taken her most of the drive home to recover from the shock. She'd insisted on our return that Spoon keep the rug in his quarters, arguing that since Spoon had found the diamond in the rough, he should be the one to enjoy it for as long as he was here.

I wondered how far Spoon could see into the future and whether he mostly only saw things that would turn out badly. When I thought back to the Black Baldy twin he'd saved by grafting and the blizzard he and I had outrun the previous winter, it sure seemed that way. But for some reason I didn't want to accept that the visions he had, especially the ones that affected me, always had to be visions of darkness. If he could envision darkness, he could surely envision light. It only made sense as far, as I was concerned, and I hoped his premonitions would take a step in that direction.

"So what's our next move?" I asked finally.

"'Fraid the next move's up to Koffman."

"Think he'd pull something underhanded?"

Spoon shrugged once again without offering either a yes or a no.

"How bad will things get?" I asked, hoping Spoon's insight might help me prepare for whatever Koffman and Acota had to offer.

"Can't say. I'll think on it. For now, why don't we call it a night?" he said, looking like someone trying his best to put a name to an unpleasant odor.

"Okay," I said, feeling defeated. Without another word, I turned and left.

As I headed back toward our house in the misty darkness, I had the feeling that Spoon knew more than he was admitting, but I couldn't be sure. I wasn't the one, after all, with the ability to see the future.

Seven

Despite my fears and Spoon's reluctance to predict how and when trouble might hit, the rest of the summer went by smoothly, except when we lost a couple of first-calf heifers in late July to what Spoon and my dad were certain was a wolf, an animal that the state Fish, Wildlife and Parks Department claimed was long gone from our region. Dad filed a report with the department, and Spoon even supplied the authorities with a plaster cast of a partial print of the phantom heifer-killer's paw. But no one took either Spoon or Dad seriously, and soon the possible wolf killings became just another rangeland myth.

By the time August and the first anniversary of Spoon's arrival rolled around, Spoon was up to his elbows researching his roots. He'd discovered that for years he'd lived under a serious misconception, thinking his paternal roots could be traced back to a 9th Cavalry buffalo soldier who had served a stint with Kit Carson at Fort Garland, Colorado, around 1879, before mustering out of the army and heading west to Montana Territory to seek his fortune. The soldier had supposedly settled first in Billings before moving on to the Bozeman region and settling in what is now known as Paradise Valley.

After numerous trips to Hardin, sometimes accompanied by my mom, who seemed insistent that Spoon solve his lineage riddle, excursions to dozens of libraries, off-the-beaten-track ranches, county courthouses, and school district headquarters, and even visits to a couple of county sheriffs' offices, including those in Butte to the west and Glasgow and Wolf Point to the north, the story of the wandering buffalo soldier unraveled. It fizzled to an end with an eighty-five-year-old former Bozeman county clerk who now lived in a small cottage on the Milk River just outside Glasgow, a town about three hundred miles northeast of our ranch. Spoon learned that her parents had actually known the former buffalo soldier and that the gruff, ebony-skinned mountain man, who'd kept to himself and lived alone in the Gallatin National Forest near Pine Creek, had never been married or fathered any children.

That news sent the normally upbeat Spoon into a tailspin that lasted until he received a postcard from the same woman informing him that she'd forgotten to mention during their meeting that, according to her now long-deceased father, the mountain man had had a friend, another former buffalo soldier who'd come to Montana Territory with him. The friend, to the best of her father's recollection and now hers, had been killed in an avalanche in the Little Belt Mountains a few years after their arrival, but not before he'd befriended several influential northern Cheyenne tribesmen who'd seemed amazed by the buffalo soldier's ability to pinpoint the elusive hiding places and winter trail routes and ranges of big game.

Spoon remained euphoric for days after the arrival of that postcard, floating on a sea of hope, convinced that he was as close to zeroing in on his heritage as he'd ever been.

When he asked me one day to ride into Hardin with him to visit the courthouse and library to check out a lead he'd gotten from a Crow woman who'd given him information about the soldier killed in the avalanche, I jumped at the chance. The woman, Spoon told me, knew an old Cheyenne man who lived off the reservation in the town of Colstrip and supposedly knew intimate details of the buffalo soldier's life and death.

As I waited on the front stoop of the bunkhouse, watching Spoon change out of a pair of muddy boots into his favorite pair of Luccheses, the boots he'd chosen the night we met, I sensed that Spoon was hanging his hat on an awful lot of hearsay and that he was setting himself up to be disappointed again. For Spoon, disappointment ignited a certain sullenness, a kind of reluctant bitterness that said to anyone observing him closely, *I've been cheated.* I'd seen that side of Spoon a year earlier, when he'd talked about his fight with the two Crows who'd tried to snooker him at cards, and two months earlier, the morning after we'd had our late-night talk about Easy Ed Koffman's intentions. That morning, I'd seen Spoon and my dad talking just outside the machine shop. The pensive look on Spoon's face and his animated gestures as much as said, *Whatever happens, don't let Koffman cheat you outta nothin', Bill.*

△ △ △

The eighteen-mile ride into Hardin in one of the ranch's ever in-need-of-repair pickups took us from the green lushness of the Willow Creek valley up onto terrain that could only be described as desolate. The hard, barren land was wedded just below the surface to a lime precipitate of caliche that ran just above the water table. I thought about Koffman as we bumped along, aware that where there was caliche, there was certainly shale, and where there was shale, its geologic cousins, coal and oil, couldn't be far away.

I'd always taken it to be a matter of happenstance that our ranch harbored so much coal. Spoon, however, had a different take. Once I'd heard Spoon suggest to my dad that our fortunes had to do with the fact that the fossils that had become our coal had met their fate by somehow getting segregated from their water source, while the desolate land we were now riding through, land rich in oil and razor-sharp shale, was in fact a far less densely fossilized area.

Despite his interest in the landscape, how it might have been formed, and its true source of precious minerals, Spoon had little use for the formal science of geology, and although he knew that I was fascinated by the science in a future-college-major way, he considered my textbook type of interest totally impractical. When I'd mentioned to him that perhaps the difference between coal being on our land and oil and shale being a greater part of the surrounding rangeland had something to do with the compacting and compressive events that had occurred during the pre-Cambrian geological era, he'd looked up at me, smiled, and said, "Don't never pay to be too much of a bookworm, TJ. Livin' in the real world always teaches you a whole lot more."

In the end, I suspected, it didn't matter how the minerals lying beneath the thousands of acres of Willow Creek grazing land had managed their way there, or for that matter what Spoon or I thought about their genesis. The bottom line was that most of the world, and Acota Energy in particular, would give its eyeteeth for the coal.

We rode most of the final leg of our trip in silence, Spoon drumming his fingers on the steering wheel and me eyeing the horizon and thinking about how to keep a foot in two worlds.

△ △ △

Hardin, a town of three thousand, moved slowly, and except for ranchers and tourists day-tripping their way into town looking for a respite from their visit to the Custer battlefield, or late-summer fly fishermen stocking up on that special fly they needed to take a trophy-sized rainbow out of the Bighorn, there was little other than July's Little Bighorn Days that could send the town into a much higher gear.

Spoon pulled the pickup, with our Triangle Long Bar brand, more than a hundred years old, stenciled in black on the front doors, into an angled parking space a few buildings down from the Big Horn County courthouse. As he stretched and adjusted his Stetson, his right arm thumped me in the chest.

"Sorry," he said. "Almost forgot you were there, you been so quiet. What's got you so preoccupied?"

"Nothing, really," I said, bending the truth, aware

that for most of the last part of our ride I'd been thinking about something my mom had said the previous evening at dinner. What she'd said, although she hadn't put it as bluntly as I'd been recalling, was that my time was up. I'd had over a year to explore every working facet of the ranch, and now that I could run the place on my own if it ever came to it, she expected that when January rolled around I'd take my reenergized body and mind and the 4-H scholarship I still had reserved for me off to the University of Montana to study geology and agriscience, as I'd always said I would.

"You'll have a leg up on most of your classmates," she'd said. "You'll be older and wiser, with a full eighteen months of insightfulness on them." The no-nonsense half smile she'd flashed had let me know that I had no more wiggle room.

When I'd looked to my dad for support, hoping he'd say, "Marva, I need the boy here," he'd remained silent. He'd had no choice. Years earlier he'd made a pact with my mom that my education would extend beyond high school and the confines of Willow Creek Ranch and that, no matter the toll on the two of them or the cost, I'd go to college. It would be hard to go back on his word to her—we both knew that, and now that Spoon was there to help keep the ranch moving along on an even keel for the first time in years, I suspected my days at Willow Creek were numbered.

The sound of Spoon swinging his door shut and his probing "Sure nothin's the matter?" moved me out of my seat.

"Nope." I jumped out of the truck, trying my best to feign excitement, and eyed the cloudless blue sky as a sudden warm late-summer breeze kissed my face. "Just wondering what kind of winter you're in for." The way I said "you're" instead of "we're" might at one time have given Spoon insight into what was bothering me, but since the search for his roots was pretty much consuming him, I was certain he'd missed the inference.

"Come on up to the courthouse with me." As was his custom, whether he'd just stepped off a horse or out of a pickup, Spoon dusted himself off. "There's always the off-chance you might learn somethin' about your own ancestry while we're there."

I nodded and followed him up the steps of the boxy-looking art deco limestone building. Inside, the courthouse, last remodeled in the 1950s, was a rabbit warren of rooms. Dark wood paneling and walls painted an unappealing mud brown soaked up most of the light. Narrow territorial-style windows and maroon Spanish-tile floors, worn smooth from nearly a century of foot traffic, only seemed to enhance the darkness. The building's saving grace was that it was cool and damp enough by virtue of its placement in the middle of a bank of water-seeking cottonwoods to make you forget that you lived in a place where the humidity often failed to reach ten percent.

I stopped to get a drink of water at the first-floor water fountain as Spoon headed for the clerk and recorder's office. When I glanced through a window facing the street, I noticed Harvey "Cain" Woodson standing a few steps away from our pickup. Thinking little of his presence, since he was a common Hardin fixture and the four-term sheriff of Big Horn County, I turned and sprinted down the hall to catch up with Spoon.

I reached the clerk and recorder's office, a room blessed with fifteen-foot ceilings and the only place in the building that seemed to have enough light, to find Spoon talking to Harriet Rankin, a plump, cherub-cheeked, auburn-haired woman in her late thirties. I suspected they'd met before during one of Spoon's earlier trips to the courthouse, but I wasn't certain. Harriet, whom I'd known all my life, was a close friend of my mom's. As Spoon flipped through the pages of a massive four-inch-thick ledger, she smiled at me and said, "Haven't seen you in a while, TJ. How are things out at the ranch?"

"Fine."

"Good. Your mom and I are planning on doing our annual canning here shortly. Expect I'll be seeing a lot more of you then, unless you're headed off to U of M, that is."

"Not 'til January." My morbid response, no more than a whisper, caught Spoon's attention. When his head shot up at the reminder I'd be leaving, hurt was evident in his eyes. As quickly as he'd looked up, he turned his attention back to the ledger, flipping through half a dozen pages before stopping at one near the middle of the book to peruse it. After staring at the page for a good thirty seconds, he looked at Harriet, then me, and hollered, "Here it is!" Thumping an index finger repeatedly on the page, he locked eyes with Harriet. "Right in black and white. Here for everyone to see."

I took a step closer to the ledger, looking down on the perfectly ruled, age-yellowed page. The date to the right of a brief handwritten paragraph just below Spoon's finger read *November 22, 1889*. I hastily read the paragraph.

Recorded this date and witnessed by my hand and with my seal as Big Horn County Clerk and Recorder, let it be known that the warranty deed appended here is valid and that the following described real estate situated in Big Horn County, State of Montana, is conveyed and warranted to wit: Township 25 north, range 69 west of the 6th P.M., Big Horn County, Montana: Eighteen acres more or less in Section 21, NE 1/4/4 NE 1/4, also known as Powder River Bluff. Grantor, Andrew Thackett, for and in consideration of One Dollar and other valuable considerations, inhand paid, conveys and warrants such land to Elijah K. Witherspoon and S. Redhawk.

The seal of the State of Montana and the John Hancock–sized signature of the county clerk and recorder occupied a space beneath Andrew Thackett's signature.

Spoon remained euphoric. "I knew it. I knew it!" A couple who'd walked in behind us smiled and nodded as if to congratulate Spoon.

Looking as wide eyed and as filled with enthusiasm as I'd seen in weeks, Spoon asked Harriet, "Can you make a copy of this page, ma'am? I'm thinkin' the people who originally purchased that land were my kin. Any chance you might be able to trace down what happened to the parcel?"

"Perhaps. But I'd have to look through decades of land sales."

"I'll pay you for it."

"No need, Mr. Witherspoon. This isn't New York City."

"Sure appreciate it, ma'am."

"And this isn't Stone Mountain, Georgia, either," said Harriet. "The *ma'am*'s not necessary." She smiled at me. "Besides, it makes me feel old."

"Then the *ma'am*'s gone for sure," Spoon said, grinning.

I had a feeling as I watched Spoon beam and Harriet play coy that if I hadn't been there, their game of cat and mouse might have gone on a stretch longer. Sensing my raised antennae, Spoon cut things short.

"I can come back and get that copy later," he said, making a pretense of leaving.

"Oh, no. It'll just take me second." Harriet hefted the cumbersome ledger and headed for a nearby document scanner. "I'll be right back."

She returned moments later and handed Spoon a photocopy. "Have you been searching for your people for a long time, Mr. Witherspoon?"

"Since I came back from Vietnam."

"That's a long time."

"Twenty years this month, to be exact, from 1971 'til now."

"A generation," I said, surprising myself with the kind of response I'd have expected from my dad.

"Sounds a lot longer when you put it like that, TJ.

No matter—I'm gettin' real close to the end."

"Good luck with the rest of your search, Mr. Witherspoon. I hope you find what you're looking for. In the meantime, I'll work on trying to track down whatever happened to that eighteen acres of land."

"I sure appreciate that. And it's Spoon."

Harriet smiled. "And I'm Harriet—without the *ma'am*."

Spoon nodded and tipped his Stetson. "Thanks so much for the help, Harriet."

"My pleasure," Harriet said, sounding like a school-girl who'd just found someone to carry her books. "And in case you hit pay dirt before I can get you that land information, let me know how your search turns out."

Spoon pivoted toward the exit with a broad grin on his face. "I'll do that," he said, glancing back over his shoulder. Uncharacteristically at a loss for more words, he stammered, "I'll do that for sure."

Eight

I couldn't tell if the bounce in Spoon's step, a lightness on his feet that began as we headed down the courthouse steps and continued as we walked down the sidewalk toward the pickup, had to do with the new lead on his roots or his encounter with Harriet Rankin. It didn't matter, really; the fact that he seemed reenergized was good enough for me. I didn't have the nerve to mention anything about his almost schoolboyish response to Harriet, but since canning season and Harriet's visits to the ranch would soon be at hand, I had the feeling that more information would soon come to light.

I didn't see Sheriff Woodson standing on the far side of our pickup near the left rear wheel well, clipping his fingernails and intermittently eyeing the crew cab's backseat, until we were almost on top of him. The look on Spoon's face when he caught sight of the sheriff, the crestfallen look of an athlete who recognizes that the odds of winning the contest that will follow are stacked against him, told me all I needed to know.

The sheriff, a big man with muttonchop sideburns, sandy crew-cut hair, and a square face, ambled to the front of the pickup, looked directly at me, and asked, "So what brings you into town, TJ, and with a visit to the courthouse, no less?" He seemed purposely to ignore Spoon.

"I came in with Spoon to check on some property records."

As Woodson looked Spoon up and down, I had the distinct feeling that if I hadn't been there he might have frisked him. Nonetheless, his response was polite. "Mr. Witherspoon," he said, clearing his throat, "I've heard you've been around for a while, helping out at Willow Creek. Pleased to finally have the chance to meet you." The sheriff touched the brim of his hat. "Harvey Woodson, Big Horn County sheriff."

Spoon nodded without answering.

Woodson stepped sideways and stroked his chin thoughtfully. His eyes never left Spoon's. "So you're checkin' out our county records. Looking for anything in particular?"

"I'm hopin' to trace down my roots. Had a great-grandfather who supposedly settled somewhere around here."

"I see. And what about the rest of your folks? They all from Ohio like you?"

Spoon seemed less surprised by the question than I was, but I was sure the sheriff could tell from the looks on our faces that we were wondering how he knew Spoon was from Ohio.

"Most of 'em," Spoon said softly.

"Great state, Ohio. Industry, agriculture, first-rate college football team. You ever play football, Spoon?"

Spoon's response was a door-slamming *No!* and although the sheriff probably didn't understand the reason that Spoon was upset, I did. He never referred to himself as Spoon, and he never let others call him by that name unless he first invited them to. I'd never heard anyone except my mother, and then only on those rare occasions when she was peeved, call him Arcus, but when he initially introduced himself, Spoon typically used his full name, Arcus Witherspoon.

I could tell from the look on his face that Spoon wanted to tell the sheriff, "It's Mr. Witherspoon." But he didn't speak, and I had the sure sense that his reluctance to do so had everything to do with the fact that I was standing there.

Woodson, who stood half a head taller than the much slimmer five-foot-eleven Spoon and an inch or so taller than me, and who outweighed either of us by a good twenty-five to thirty pounds, took a step toward us and edged his left hand along the side rail of the pickup. I'd never seen Spoon look so intimidated.

"You ever own land back in Ohio, Spoon?" Woodson asked, his earlier politeness on the wane.

"Where you headed with this, Sheriff?" Spoon asked.

Woodson flashed a toothy grin. "I'm headed where any law enforcement officer should be headed, given your presence in *our* county and now *our* courthouse, Spoon."

Spoon stood stone faced and motionless as we both considered the sheriff's choice of words. The way he'd said *our* made it sound as if Spoon had no right to be there. When Woodson finally turned his attention to me, his tone was condescending.

"Seems your hired hand here had himself some problems with the law in the past, TJ. Got himself into a conflict over, of all things, a piece of land back in Ohio.

It's been several years back, right, Spoon?" Woodson said, clearly not expecting an answer. "The story I got is that when the Preble County assessor slapped a tax lien on a forty-acre parcel with a run-down old cabin on it, land that your hired man here claimed to own, Spoon beat the poor deputy sheriff who delivered the lien half to death. To make matters worse, and this is according to law enforcement people I talked to back in Ohio, when a second deputy showed up to evict Spoon from the property and make an arrest, they came close to havin' a shootout." Woodson cracked a wry smile. "I'm guessin' neither you nor your pa knew that Mr. Witherspoon here served eighteen months in the Ohio State Pen."

I glanced at Spoon, pleading with my eyes for him to offer a rebuttal, but his only response was the brief, icy stare he flashed Woodson.

Rocking back on his heels and looking self-satisfied, Woodson said to Spoon, "So I guess you can see my predicament and why we're havin' this little chat. Especially since I've got myself what might be described as a similar situation to the one in Ohio right here in Big Horn County—an ex-con searchin' out property records at *my* county courthouse. Wouldn't want a repeat of what happened back in the Buckeye State. So know this, Spoon. Things get handled a lot different out here than they do in Ohio. The law's less lenient, and people have been known to get busted up, even shot at, over as minor a matter as a half inch of water height on a weir."

Spoon's response caught me by surprise. "Yeah, I know. Like over coal."

"That too," said Woodson, breaking into the toothy grin again. Removing his hand from the railing, he lowered it to the butt of his holstered 9-millimeter. "So consider yourself warned." His thumb lingered briefly on the gun butt. "I don't want one ounce of any carpetbagging trouble out of you, Spoon. Are we straight on that?"

Spoon brushed the sheriff aside with a look of disdain, turned to me without answering, and asked, "Ready to head back to the ranch, TJ?"

"Yes," I said, trying my best not to look nervous.

"Pleasure talkin' to you, Sheriff," Spoon said, his expression unchanged. He took a step back, swung the pickup door open, and slipped behind the wheel as I moved to get in on the passenger's side. Poking an elbow out of the truck's open window in clear finger-pointing defiance, Spoon said, "There's lots of people around your county lookin' to get their hands on other folks' land, or what's under it, Sheriff. I'm thinkin' maybe you should be talkin' to them instead of me. I'm just a man in search of his roots." He flashed Woodson one of his penetrating, trancelike, all-knowing looks before cranking the engine. "But then again, you and them land-grabbers I just mentioned are all probably real good friends."

Before Woodson, his face now salmon pink, could respond, Spoon backed the pickup into the street and pointed it toward home.

△ △ △

Halfway back to the ranch we hit the leading edge of a thunderstorm packed with streaming white ground-to-sky stepladder lightning so intense and so heavy with rain that Spoon had to pull the pickup to a stop along the shoulder of the county road to wait it out. As thunderclaps exploded around us, I hesitantly asked, "What really happened back in Ohio?" hoping Spoon's answer wouldn't jibe with the sheriff's account.

Looking thoughtfully serene, Spoon said, "We'll talk about it later when I have your ma and pa there to hear me out as well. Okay?" His words had the weight of a court-case-closing gavel.

"Yeah," I said, sorry I'd asked. I had the sense as the storm let up and we continued on that Spoon didn't much enjoy being ambushed by anyone, regardless of whether it was some small-town sheriff or me. From the nervous way he kept fidgeting with his seatbelt and adjusting his Stetson, I also got the feeling that something was eating at him that was far more troubling than any past transgression.

When I caught sight of our ranch house in the hazy distance, I knew two things for certain: Spoon's prediction about trouble on the horizon for our family had just weighed in at a hundred percent, and I'd never blindside him with an impertinent question again.

△ △ △

The suppertime powwow that evening turned out to be frank talk around a dinner table overflowing with food

that included my mom's homemade biscuits and straw-
berry preserves, fresh string beans and summer squash
from her garden, mashed potatoes and gravy, and melt-in-
your-mouth, two-and-a-half-inch-thick steaks from one
of the prior year's butchered calves. It was the kind of talk
that would never have occurred with me sitting there if it
hadn't been for my mom's dogged insistence.

I'd told her what had happened in Hardin soon
after Spoon and I had gotten back to the ranch, thinking
her level-headed assessment might be helpful. Later, she
approached the two of us as we were repairing a temperamental lamppost in front of our house and asked Spoon
about our encounter with the sheriff. He flashed me a dis-
heartened look and said, "I was plannin' on takin' that up
with Bill and you later, Mrs. D."

Taking in the crestfallen look on Spoon's face, my
mom eyed me protectively and moved a half-filled bucket
of blackberries from her right hip to her left. "Don't look
at TJ so disapprovingly. He only wants to help. We've all
got our stories, Arcus Witherspoon, sad ones and happy
ones and those we aren't particularly proud of. I'm not
sure whether you knew it or not, but I was once a profes-
sional dancer, and a damn good one at that. I left that life
behind for a heck of a good man who had his heart set on
working the land you see around you." She set the blackberries down and swung her arm in a wide 180-degree
arc. "Land that's become as much a part of me as it has
always been for him."

The look of intensity on her face had me wondering
if she might not be coming down too hard on Spoon.

"You've been here over a year now, Spoon, and you should know better than most that at Willow Creek Ranch we try our best to act as one unit."

She looked out toward one of our lush green treeless mesas. "I've put up hay on this place when it's been one hundred three degrees and the tractor seat beneath me seemed close to blistering. I've irrigated tens of thousands of acres on my own. I've won awards with my cutting horses and pulled stubborn, reluctant calves into this world in subzero temperatures at three in the morning."

Her gaze moved down to Willow Creek. "And I've lost a son on this place. I'm tougher than I look, Spoon, and hopefully as caring. I detest laggards and liars, and during my time in New York City I served up justice using my fists to more than one overmatched, unsuspecting letch. So we'll talk about what happened in town at supper this evening. All four of us, like people who have concern for one another. After that, if you and Bill need to talk in private, take the whole night."

She didn't wait for a response. Instead she picked up her blackberries, turned, and walked back toward the house. I expected that Spoon might have felt offended, but a few hours later he was sitting at our dining room table. The vase of wildflowers he'd brought my mom served as that night's centerpiece.

Spoon was wrapping up telling us about what had really happened in Ohio as I piled a second coating of blackberries onto what was left of a bowl of homemade vanilla ice cream and listened intently. His tone was a bit sad and uncharacteristically apologetic.

"So when that land-grabbin' deputy sheriff came after me, swingin' the business end of a shovel in one hand and a ten-pound sledgehammer in the other, screamin' that the sheriff would show up next and shoot me if he had to, I hit him with the tree limb I'd picked up. I never beat him to a pulp like it said in the newspapers. Never did much more than give him a goose egg on his head and a shiner. But the newspapers and a couple of local TV stations decided to have a field day with what happened. Played it up like I was some kinda stressed-out post–Vietnam War deranged animal. And I didn't do myself no good pickin' a fight with a good ol' boy. Turns out that piece of land I thought I owned, goin' all the way back to a great-uncle, had been picked up at a tax sale by the cousin of the guy I thumped with the tree limb."

Spoon let out a sigh and continued. "Got myself a public defender to try and help me outta the jam, 'cause I couldn't afford no real honest-to-goodness lawyer. He was a skinny little Irish boy who couldn'ta been outta Ohio State's law school more than a coupla years. The kid turned out to be one of the most principled men I ever met, and smart as a whip. Smart enough to keep me from servin' five to ten. The first time I met him, even before he asked me if I'd really clobbered Mr. Ellis McCabe like folks on TV were sayin', he asked me whether I'd ever gotten any tax notices about the piece of property in dispute. When I told him no, I'd never gotten a dang-gone thing, he shook his head and said, 'Par for the course—nobody ever does.' I didn't understand what he meant by that remark until a whole lot later.

"I was ten months into servin' a three-year term when it came down that my lawyer had uncovered a landgrab scam that had been cooked up by a group of tax lien schemers and the Preble County sheriff. A plan designed to hoodwink ignorant, mostly outta-state landowners and a few targeted Vietnam veterans like me who'd been outta circulation for a while. It took my lawyer another seven months to work my case up to the point that a judge would have another look at it, and by then I'd done close to eighteen months. Lucky for me, it was just about that time that *The Cincinnati Enquirer* started runnin' an investigative piece on the whole landgrab scam. One that ended up makin' mincemeat outta the people who'd set me up. So with the aid of a damn good lawyer, a newspaper lookin' for a story, and public opinion on my side, I walked outta prison three days short of servin' eighteen months behind bars. I left Ohio the next week and don't never plan on returnin'. That is, unless they offer me a full pardon instead of labelin' my situation a face-savin' mistrial."

I dropped my spoon onto my bowl, and, except for the loud clank, there was hushed silence at the table. Finally my mom said, "So you started working your way west."

"Did just that," said Spoon. "Decided I needed to track down the person who'd supposedly left my uncle and me heir on that land. All I had to go on was that my great-grandfather had been in the army right after the Civil War, that he was stationed out west, and that he married an Indian woman. You pretty much know things from there."

Looking like someone who'd just bared his soul, Spoon said, "I can pack on outta here if need be. Don't do good folks like you a whole lotta good havin' an ex-con workin' for 'em."

"I decide who works for me," my dad said.

Spoon nodded, then looked at my mom as if he expected her to add her yea or nay. She simply offered him a supportive smile and said, "There's more pie in the kitchen if anybody wants some."

When everyone turned to look at me, I said, "If it had been Willow Creek caught up in a landgrab like that, I just might've killed that Mr. McCabe."

My mom's eyes widened in horror, but my dad simply nodded in agreement.

We finished our meal, draining a freshly brewed pot of hazelnut coffee. After finishing his second cup, Spoon looked at me and said in a quizzical voice that seemed to rise from deep in his gut, "Sheriff Woodson was pretty raw in his approach today, wouldn't you say, TJ?"

"Sure would."

"And wouldn't you say he seemed to know an awful lot about me that I sure as blazes never told him?"

"Yeah."

Spoon set his coffee cup aside and stared at me thoughtfully. "So where on earth do you think he got his inside dope? More important, and I shoulda asked him this when he was busy grillin' me, how'd he know we'd be in town today, much less exactly where to find us?"

"I guess he saw our pickup. Hard to miss the Triangle Long Bar brand."

"Possible. But that woulda had him spendin' a lot of time cruisin' around lookin' for our vehicle." Spoon eyed my dad. "Whatta you think, Bill?"

My dad swallowed hard, as if something were lodged in his throat. "I'd say he had a little prior knowledge you were comin'. A lot of folks claim that badge of Cain Woodson's can sometimes be for sale."

"That'd be my take too," said Spoon, nodding in agreement.

"But to whom?" asked my mom.

"That's the sixty-four-thousand-dollar question, Mrs. D.," said Spoon. "Any of you seen anybody suspicious lurkin' around the ranch or had the feelin' that somebody's watchin' our comin's and goin's?"

"Not me," I said quickly.

"Nothing," Mom and Dad said in near unison.

In a strangely omniscient voice, Spoon said, "Well, keep your eyes out. Sooner or later they'll pop up."

"You think we're under surveillance?" my mom asked with disbelief.

"Yep."

"Why?"

We all eyed my mom, aware of the answer, and although she'd been the one to ask the question, she no doubt knew the answer as well. The muscles in her forehead tightened. My dad simply looked angry as, with both elbows planted firmly on the table, Spoon whispered, "Coal."

Nine

Two days after Spoon's confessional supper, word spread throughout the valley that Rulon and Beatrice Demaster had sold out to Acota. In truth, they'd simply leased Acota the rights to strip-mine their nine thousand acres for a period of fifteen years. Long regarded by many valley old-timers as interlopers, the reclusive husband-and-wife team had now become pariahs.

A few of our valley's smaller ranchers, however, viewed the Demasters' lease agreement as a blessing that had the potential to blow a windfall their way. No matter your persuasion, the deal Acota had struck with the Demasters had the potential to ultimately pit neighbor against neighbor.

Rumor spread that Acota, now that it had its foot in the door, planned to refuse to negotiate with any landowner who couldn't guarantee it at least a section to mine, which meant that the half dozen or so ranchers with less than 640 acres to throw in the pot would be left out in the cold. Three ranches, including ours, appeared to be pots of coal-rich gold.

The Demasters didn't show up at the hastily called meeting at Willard Johnson's ranch the evening after word leaked out that Acota was concentrating on cementing deals with the three largest remaining ranches in the valley, but everyone else was there. Dale Turpin, a widower whose family had ranched in our valley for over a hundred years, was talking to everyone in his high-pitched, squeaky voice and wearing his trademark checkerboard shirt and baggy overalls. The Cundiffs, Ralph and Maxine, hardworking, slightly paranoid, salt-of-the-earth types who scratched out a living on two thousand acres and who I considered had the most to gain, showed up fifteen minutes late for the meeting, looking harried and nervous as hell. A dozen other people representing six other valley ranches were also there, but it was Turpin, the Cundiffs, Willard Johnson, and my family who had control of the show.

My mom, always at ease in a crowd, chatted amiably with everyone while my dad and I stood off to the side and Spoon mingled much like my mom. In the year since he'd come to Willow Creek, he'd become a fixture in our valley. He'd helped everyone at the gathering in some way at one time or another, from pulling frostbitten Ralph Cundiff's stranded pickup out of a snowbank in subzero weather to helping dig out Willard Johnson's frozen water line. Behind his back and on the strength of his uncanny ability to remedy a bad situation, generally before anyone else could even appreciate it, some people had taken to calling Spoon the black Houdini.

In the days following our encounter with Sheriff Woodson outside the Hardin courthouse, word had leaked out that Spoon had had troubles back in his home state of Ohio and that he'd spent time in prison for assaulting a man who'd tried to snooker him out of his land. Just about everyone had supported Spoon's actions, arguing that although Spoon had probably chosen the wrong response at the time, the other man had probably had it coming.

As I watched Spoon in animated conversation with Willard Johnson, he looked comfortably at home. Willard, stoop shouldered, balding, and not as clear eyed as he'd once been, was nonetheless as fit as any sixty-one-year-old I'd ever known. As folks milled around in the half-acre patch of Kentucky bluegrass next to Willard's century-old territorial-style house, chatting leisurely and drinking lemonade and beer, I had the uneasy feeling that the evening might not end so serenely.

Willard initiated the proceedings a few minutes later by slamming his sunburned right hand down on one of three collapsible picnic tables dotting the yard and announcing, "Might as well get this bus a-movin'." He slipped a piece of chaw, the rough-cut kind that he always seemed to have nestled between his lower lip and gums, from one side of his mouth to the other. "No need for beatin' 'round the bush. Everyone knows why we're here, and I'll tell you flat out that some of us larger producers are up against it."

"We're all up against it," squeaked Dale Turpin. "Unequal shares of trouble doesn't mean there's no trouble there."

My mom nodded in agreement, aware that although Dale's potential loss of the use of his land, disruption of his cattle operation, and scarring of his pristine, perpetually green, subirrigated four thousand acres couldn't equal Willard Johnson's loss, proportionately and aesthetically their losses would likely be the same.

"Didn't mean to disrespect you there, Turp," said Willard.

"No harm, no foul," Dale said. "Let's get on with it."

"Okay. Bottom line in all that's happened around here over the past week comes down to whether we're gonna unite to keep those money-grubbin' earth turners from Acota outta our valley or not. We've all heard from 'em at one time or another. Postcards, letters, phone calls, even some personal visits." Willard eyed my folks, who were seated across the table from him. "And uninvited ones at that."

"Yeah, yeah, yeah. We know all that, Willard. But whether we like it or not, thanks to the Demasters, they're in here now," said Tommy Lotus, a less-than-five-hundred-acre operator who was slouched in his seat at the head of the table closest to Willard.

"Tommy's right," Maxine Cundiff chimed in. "In spite of how they got into our shorts, and regardless of whether the Demasters opened the floodgates, what we need here, goddamnit, is a solution." She punctuated the remark with her own hand slap on the table.

I'd never much cared for the Cundiffs, Maxine in particular. Maybe it was because she drank and cursed, rolled her own cigarettes, and never failed to interrupt people's conversations. Or maybe it was because for some reason she'd always seemed jealous of my mom. Nonetheless, her take on the situation was hard to dispute. Most heads in the audience began nodding as my folks both leaned forward in their seats, but not every head, and certainly not Spoon's. He and I had remained standing next to an old ninety-weight oil drum Willard used for burning trash.

Resting my forearm on the lip of the drum, I realized that if things weren't handled right, we'd be in for a long, disruptive evening. My dad must have recognized the same thing because he spoke up immediately.

"Let's slow down here a second and make sure everyone's on the same page," he said, rising from his chair. "Acota has money to offer—bank vaults full of it, in fact. There's no debatin' that. And no matter the size of our individual operations, there's also no debatin' that we could all use an infusion of cash. But what binds us together," he said, eyeing Maxine as if he weren't quite certain she'd believe him, "is our desire to keep Acota from turning this valley into a string of strip-mining pits, a concentration camp of dust and fumes."

"Strong rhetoric for someone with the fuckin' most to gain," said Maxine, watching her husband's head hinge back and forth in agreement. "What could you Darleys possibly resent about Acota descendin' on us except maybe havin' to wait a little longer for your money?"

My dad, as quick with words as Maxine, gritted his teeth to control his tongue and his temper. Assessing looks on the faces of the rest of the ranchers assembled, he said, "What I'm holdin' out for, Maxine, is a way to preserve my way of life. A way of life I love and one I damn sure don't intend to let go."

Whenever my dad punctuated his sentences with words like *damn* or *hell*, I knew his frustration level had reached its limit. Eyeing my mom and then Spoon, who were equally aware of the idiosyncrasy and who both looked worried, I hoped Maxine was finished with her needling.

When Thurston Lyle, a thin-haired weasel of a man who decades earlier had lost most of the fingers of his left hand to the teeth of a hay baler, chimed in, saying, "Maxine's got a point," it was clear that the smaller land-owners were lining up to temper the voices of the larger ones. Thurston went on in his perpetually hoarse three-packs-a-day voice, amid mumbling and whispers at the three tables, "I say we create somethin' like a co-op, pool our resources equivalent to what we got to gain, and push back against them Acota mothers. Don't mean I'm givin' up my right to act as an individual, though, and—"

My mom interrupted, "Sorry to cut you off, Thurston, but I've got a problem with your stance. I'm not at all in favor of us sticking together until somebody decides to run off on their own, and that sounds like what you're proposing. Seems like, using your model, we'd be pooling our resources to fight off the wolves while letting anybody defect whenever they felt like it. No, I don't like your take on things one bit."

"You got a better one? Spit it out," said Thurston.

"I do. One that can be looked at and thought through by someone who knows more about these things than us. I say we adopt a co-op plan, more or less, just like you said, but only if we get ourselves a lawyer and have him look into all our legal options. Meanwhile, everybody contributes to our legal costs equally. That should take care of people running out on their own."

I wasn't certain how people would respond to my mom's suggestion, but Willard Johnson quickly offered up his point of view.

"Marva's right, and I don't mind payin' my share of the freight as long as I get my money's worth," he boomed. "Me and my kin been tendin' this land for over a hundred years. And believe me, I understand what makes it happy and what turns it sour. You can be certain that them bastards from Acota don't know a damn thing about me or my land." Willard's eyes slowly met those of everyone at the three tables. His eyes narrowed, and his lower lip began to quiver. "I'd kill over this land. No question about it." He slammed a fist into his right palm. "Got nothin' more to say on the issue."

Willard's pronouncement triggered a silence that lasted until my dad asked, "So, who gets the lawyer?"

"Why not you, Bill?" Maxine Cundiff said, eager as always to drop the heavy lifting on someone else's shoulders. "You're the one here with the most legal contacts."

"No problem," said my dad. "If everyone here agrees, I'll be happy to deal with the issue." He smiled and adjusted his Stetson as if to say, *Touché.* "That way we get us an agreement hammered out that doesn't allow for any self-servin' loopholes."

Only afterward, on the ride home, when my mom pointed out that the sooner the coalition had a lawyer, the sooner Maxine could gain insight into what might benefit her and Ralph the most, did I fully appreciate that the Cundiffs, more than anyone else because of the size of their place, would enjoy the benefit of possibly playing both ends against the middle.

"Fine by me," Maxine said, eyeing her husband and sounding uncustomarily embarrassed. "I'm for lettin' Bill line up the legal side of things. Can I get a show of like-thinkin' hands?"

Hands at all three tables quickly went up.

"Looks like it's your baby, Bill," Willard Johnson said, flashing my dad a glad-it ain't-me kind of grin.

Dad's response was a noticeably reluctant "Okay."

"Who you thinkin' about usin' to represent us?" asked Willard.

"Ricky Peterson, more than likely."

"Good." Willard looked pleased. "We can use some-body with both criminal and corporate shenanigans expertise."

When Willard glanced briefly in Spoon's direction, I had the strangest sense that for some reason they were momentarily connected. When Willard added, "'Cause like I said earlier, I'll kill over this here land," I knew they were.

△ △ △

Fifteen minutes later everyone had said their good-byes, leaving only Spoon and my folks and I to walk slowly through a field of dew-covered timothy hay and clover back to our pickup. Spoon stopped to look up at the moon. "Always looks like a perfect white pearl up there in the center of the sky when it's full on a crystal-clear night like this, don't it?"

"Sure does," I said as we all stopped.

My parents nodded in agreement.

"You can barely make out its flaws," Spoon added.

"Can't see the craters or the mountains. And there's almost nothin' to suggest the old girl's taken tens of thousands of meteor hits. She's a lot like most people, I suspect. Get far enough away from 'em and somehow you just don't see their flaws, especially when you're focusin' in on somethin' in common. But it's wise to never forget about them flaws, no matter how rosy the picture might get, wouldn't you say?"

My mom and dad glanced knowingly at one another without saying a word as, now a few steps ahead of everyone else, I jogged for the pickup, aware that Spoon's words were not only timely, but right on the mark.

Ten

By midmorning the next day, the winds had kicked up and the sky had become a thin, milky white veneer of lenticular clouds. It was on that morning that I first saw the horseman in gray. At least that was my initial name for him. He appeared about thirty yards away from me as I sat on horseback on the edge of the angling quarter-mile length of section fence that separated our ranch from Willard Johnson's. I was protected from his view by a twenty-foot-high rock outcropping. At the point where I spotted him, the fence angled straight just before dead-dropping down a steep dry wash with a thin granular overburden of soil that disguised a subsurface layer of pink feldspar, mica, and clear-as-glass quartz. My dad liked to point out that that particular part of the ranch was made up of a kind of historic land that was geologically identical to the ground west of Laramie in which the Union Pacific rail bed had been laid.

But on this day, I knew my dad wasn't contemplating history. He'd spent most of the early morning in his cramped cedar-paneled office calculating the out-of-pocket dollars he expected each member of what he was now calling the Willow Creek Ranchers Coalition to have to shell out for legal advice and representation. He'd arrived at a figure before I'd left to ride fence, and although it wasn't a perfect picture of expenses, or at the moment an equally shared expense for every coalition member, I'd heard him tell my mom it was the best he could come up with.

A little later I'd taken off on horseback to the east. Spoon had left a little earlier on a similar mission, mending fences and checking for strays in more hilly country to the west. I was half a mile away from our house when I saw my dad's pickup head down the road toward Billings. I suspected that his problem of arriving at a fair financial equation was related to the fact that the coal burden on the individual ranch lands in the valley wasn't all that equal. But when push came to shove, I suspected he could get people to modify their thinking. He'd done so himself, after all, when it came to Spoon, and although he'd inherited a job he didn't necessarily want, I expected that his stick-to-itiveness would see him through.

When I was younger, I'd often wondered where the tenacity that allowed him to ford a river at high water on horseback or rope and subdue an angry stubborn bull came from. I'd been close to thirteen when an old navy buddy of his, a man who'd served alongside him in Korea, had shown up at the ranch and offered me lasting insight into my dad's makeup. We were sitting around an early evening post-fly-fishing campfire in a swampy, subirrigated part of the ranch, near the spot where Willow Creek intersects the Bighorn River, when the man whispered to me, "Your old man's a war hero, you know. Earned himself a Navy Cross one winter during the war by abandonin' the safety of his road construction half-track, mannin' a machine gun, and tendin' to a wounded gunner's mate. Your dad took out damn near a whole platoon of North Koreans and saved my bacon. He ever tell you about that?"

When I answered no, the man smiled. "Wouldn'ta expected that he would. Braggin's not the kind of juice that's ever fueled him."

I'd never mentioned to my dad what his navy buddy had said about him, but sometimes when he looked tired, haggard, and a bit slumped in the saddle, I imagined him sprawled out, belly in the dirt, machine gun blazing, gritting his teeth and looking obstinate, determined to never give in.

Thoughts of my father faded as I continued to watch the horseman. I could see now that in addition to being dressed head to toe in gray, he was wearing a Civil War–style Johnny Reb cap. As the big black mare he was riding loped along the fence line, I could tell from the way horse and rider moved as one that the man in the saddle knew what he was doing. I wasn't certain if he'd seen me or not, positioned as I was just behind the leading edge of that rock outcropping, but if he had, nothing about his manner suggested it.

When he pulled his horse to a halt and looked due east into the sun, my heart changed rhythm, but I couldn't explain why since I'd seen Willard Johnson's hired man ride the same stretch of land scores of times over the years. Generally I stopped to chat with Rawdy Themes, but today there was only the man in gray.

I followed the horseman's trek along the fence line, never taking my eyes off him. He brought the horse to a halt, looked around as if he suddenly had the sense he was being watched, and then urged the mare quickly down a sage-covered hill. At the hill's bottom he eased the horse up, dismounted, and led her around a cattle guard that separated our land from Johnson's.

I briefly thought about riding down to tell him he'd crossed onto our property, but recalling my dad's war buddy's comments about his actions in Korea, I chose instead to hold my position.

The man in gray continued his encroachment, leading his mare toward a flat, square, marshy spit of land about three times the size of a big city intersection. It was rimmed on all sides by a wide thicket of parched brown grass and sagging barbed-wire fence that was surrounded by a dozen or so acres of land that had been in a grass fire years earlier. The fire had been started by my brother, Jimmy, and his best friend and current counselor for the Willow Creek Ranchers Coalition, Ricky Peterson.

The year before Jimmy had died, a month or so after he'd turned fifteen, he and Ricky had been out on horseback exploring the eastern edge of the ranch on a mission to eliminate as many Wyoming ground squirrels and plague-carrying western prairie dogs as they could. They'd both been packing .22 Winchesters. They'd come up on the area the horseman in gray now seemed so interested in and decided, according to my mom's account, to check out the fenced-off marshy patch, with its concealing dry rim of grass, for the vermin they were after. They'd begun stomping down the area for rodents, as was their custom, and popping them with their .22s when Ricky spotted what he thought was a tunnel near the far northern edge of the parcel and jogged toward it. With Jimmy a good ten yards or so behind him, Ricky took out the cigarette lighter he always carried to try for a better look at what he could now see was a three-by-three-foot hole in the ground. That hole, which turned out to be just one of the surface fingers of our natural gas seep, erupted immediately in flame. By Jimmy's account, Ricky was only trapped in the fire for seconds, but he sustained second- and third-degree burns to the upper half of his body that kept him hospitalized for weeks and in rehabilitation for months.

Days after the accident, my dad refenced off the patch of land and plugged up what he could of the seep's natural gas, but he left the charred fence posts standing and planted a metal warning sign just beyond the eastern boundary of the fence. That sign, rusted from age and more burnt orange now than its original yellow, still read Danger.

When the horseman in gray walked his horse within a few feet of the sign, my mouth suddenly went dry. Slapping the horse on the neck and looping the reins around a charred post as if to say, *This'll only take a second*, he jumped the fence and walked the gas seep's inner perimeter. For the next few minutes he crisscrossed the seep, kicking over rocks, examining handfuls of dirt, and picking wildflowers as his horse browsed the dry marginal grasses. I had the feeling that he was about done with his exploration when he stooped down and started rooting around in the dirt with a stick he'd picked up. I wondered as I watched him if he might not be looking for the very tunnel that Ricky had found, but when he tossed the stick aside, I wasn't so certain.

Seconds later he was back over the fence, and as agile as a gymnast he was quickly back on his horse. When the horse looked around and sniffed into the wind as if she'd caught a hint of something foreboding, the man in gray did the same. I leaned forward in my saddle and whispered, "Don't you dare snort," to my eight-year-old gelding, Dusty.

When both horse and rider seemed content that there was no immediate threat, they took off at a trot back up the hill they'd descended earlier. The trot soon turned into a gallop. When the big black mare jumped the cattle guard that separated Johnson's property from ours, I mumbled, "Shit," and when the horse made a sharp turn to the south, I saw something I either hadn't noticed or hadn't been able to see earlier. Poking out from a scabbard that ran diagonally across the horse's left hindquarter was the stock of a rifle. Not the narrow stock of a .22, for dealing with pesky varmints, but the larger stock of what I suspected was a .30-'06, with firepower enough to take out a deer or elk, or even a man.

A ground-hugging trail of dust rose from behind the galloping rider as he moved farther away, and I wondered as he disappeared over a rise why on earth he'd been trespassing on both Willard Johnson's land and ours, why he needed a high-powered rifle, and if he perhaps worked for Acota Energy and Ed Koffman. But most of all I wondered whether he was aware that the northern face of the bluffs that rose above the fenced-off natural gas seep, the very bluffs I'd been hiding in, were no more than the thin, rocky veneer over a flat-topped mountain of coal.

△ △ △

I was still pondering what I'd seen at our natural gas seep when I met up with Spoon several hours later. I'd decided not to tell him about the trespassing rider until we were home. We were heading across our thirteen-hundred-acre Marva pasture, named in honor of my mom, a pasture that always blossomed with a sea of buttercups in the late spring, when Dusty, aware that we were headed home, reared his head without instruction. When I thumped him hard on the neck with two fingers, exasperated that I'd never been able to break him of the bad habit, Spoon laughed. It wasn't his usual booming laugh but one that seemed halfhearted.

"He knows there's a brush-down and grain awaitin'. Besides, he knows every square foot of this place. He can spot the end of a work day quick as any human. They're thinkers, not just beasts of burden, TJ."

Spoon had plenty of proof to back him up. Months earlier when Duke, my dad's blue heeler, had cornered a fence-jumping yearling steer that I'd been trying to vaccinate, holding the steer in place, trancelike and motionless, until Spoon appeared on horseback to rope him, I'd had the sense that Spoon understood animals on some plane that I couldn't possibly appreciate.

"Them two animals are just talkin' to one another," he'd called out to me, taking up the slack in his rope. "Problem is, we're too dumb to understand their language." He then let out a strange yelp as if to say to both horse and dog, *Good show*, dismounted, took the syringe out of my hand, and vaccinated the suddenly docile yearling.

We didn't get back to headquarters until close to five o'clock. As Spoon dismounted, removed his sweat-stained Stetson, and swiped his brow with the cuff of his shirt, he looked tired. When he looped his horse's reins around one of the iron-pipe hitching posts in front of our barn, I knew from the look on his face that he'd had trouble that day. I wondered if he'd also run across the trespassing man in gray and questioned whether holding back on my own sighting had been a mistake.

"Something the matter, Spoon?"

"Nope. Just had myself a bad day."

"What happened?"

"Fell off my horse. Landed on my noggin. Sorta went cuckoo for a little bit."

"How'd you do that?"

"Got to chasin' one of them ornery Angus bulls of Willard Johnson's who decided he'd come over on us. I was runnin' him through a willow thicket back toward home when I didn't take notice of a tree. Tree limb caught me in the neck and sent me spinnin'. Got my maker to thank for the patch of sandy soil I landed in, and of course my rock-hard noggin. Never did find out what happened to that bull. Guess he ran laughin' back over to Johnson's." Spoon shook his head as if to rid himself of any lingering cobwebs. "How'd your day go? We got any fence problems out east?"

"Nothing but a few popped top wires. I fixed 'em. And just one stray. Took me a while, but I moved her back in with her sorority sisters."

When Spoon finally moved close enough for me to see the massive welt above his right ear, I said, "That's one hell

of a knot you've got there," suspecting now that he was trying his best to mask a concussion and considerable pain.

"Coulda been worse," he said, unsaddling his horse
while I moved to unsaddle Dusty.

He headed for the barn's tack room, saddle on his left
shoulder, as I slipped a halter on Dusty. When he came
back he was holding grooming brushes in both hands. As
we brushed the horses down, I said, "Something strange
happened to me today too," trying my best to sound matter of fact.

"You take a spill too?"

"Nope. Ran across a trespasser."

The instant I said "trespasser," Spoon's eyes widened,
curtains lifting on the opening act of a play. "Where was
he?"

"Over by the fenced-off natural gas seep of ours that
caught fire years ago," I said.

Spoon's next question wasn't about the trespasser or
how I'd spotted him, or even about what had happened
after my sighting. Instead he asked, "Your pa come back
from seein' that lawyer in Billings yet?"

"Nope."

"He tell you what time his appointment was?"

"No."

"Wish he had."

"You're talking in riddles, Spoon. Am I missing
something?"

Spoon simply smiled. The smile came slowly, as if for
some reason, in the wake of his tumble, smiling made his
head hurt. Finally he said, "Yep. You are. There's a connection

between that natural gas seep, your pa bein' gone all day, and that trespasser."

When he realized from the confused look on my face that he'd left me adrift somewhere outside his prophetic world, he said, "I'll explain things to you later. Right now why you don't tell me about that trespasser, and don't leave nothin' out. I wanna hear about things exactly the way they happened."

Eleven

For as long as I could remember, the rusted old hand-primed well pump inside our barn had been temperamental. One day it spewed water like Victoria Falls; the next it barely put out a stream. On days when my dad had a lot on his mind or when life seemed to simply be dogging him, he'd pull out the battered red metal case that held his plumbing tools and he'd go to work on that pump. My mom always claimed that the problem wasn't with the pump, but with the well and that if he'd just drill a new well, the problem would solve itself. But Dad, his stubbornness always at its zenith when it came to that pump, would lay out his pipe wrenches, spirit cleaners, grease, copper snips, and pipe threaders and go at that pump, sometimes for hours, until in the end the pump would again, at least temporarily, gush water.

Fixing that pump was therapy for him, both mental and physical, and that was why neither my mom nor I belabored the issue of sinking a new well and why my dad never called for a drilling rig to come sink one.

Dad was down on his knees with the old pump housing, absent its handle, lying beside him when I approached him to tell him about our trespasser. It was just past dark, and the echoey, bat-infested, two-and-a-half-story, eighty-six-year-old barn, the oldest building on the ranch, was creaking. The building's lighting had been upgraded only once since my grandfather and his neighbors had built the double widow-peaked behemoth in a barn-raising marathon that had lasted less than seven days from start to finish. With its dozen livestock stalls, their wooden top rails chewed to the quick by horses, generous tack room, propane-fired warming room for newborn calves, and temperamental well, the barn was something of a conversation piece in the valley.

The rough-cut timbered supports and sawdust-covered floor had always given my sinuses fits, and within moments of stepping inside, I could guarantee a bout of sneezing. It never lasted for more than a few minutes before subsiding, and the half dozen doctors I'd seen for the problem since childhood had agreed that what I was most likely suffering from was an immediate but temporary sawdust allergy. Although the sneezing passed quickly, it was a nuisance that had always made me weary, if not a bit fearful, of the drafty old relic.

My first sneeze caught my dad off guard, and when his head snapped around toward me, he nearly dropped his pipe wrench. "TJ, you startled the hell out of me," he said, regripping the wrench.

"Sorry."

He quickly went back to assembling the pump handle, picking up a four-inch bolt and rolling it back and forth in the palm of one hand before inserting it into the pump handle's throat support. Shaking his head, he said, "You know, your mom might be right. I'm thinkin' we probably would be better off with a new well." He eyed the reassembled pump handle, then looked up at me for affirmation.

"Could be, but wells cost money, so if this old dog of ours can still hunt, I say we keep using it."

Dad smiled, surprised by my use of one of his favorite sayings.

"That's always been my take," he said, tightening down the bolt.

I eyed the backs of his badly sunburned hands and his gnarled, twice-broken middle fingers, and found myself wondering if during his time in Korea he'd ever had to use his hands to kill someone, when suddenly he asked, "So what's so important that it brings you out here for a bout of sneezin'?"

"Something I saw today while I was out riding fence," I said, getting straight to the point. "A trespasser on horseback. He was riding a big black mare, dressed head to toe in gray, and believe it or not, he was sporting one of those Johnny Reb caps. He was on Willard Johnson's place before he rode down onto ours. Watched him for a good half hour before he took off."

"Where'd you see him?"

"Down by the natural gas seep where Ricky Peterson got burned."

My dad's half nod let me know he was only slightly surprised by my revelation. "What was he doing?"

"Checking things out. Taking in the lay of the land, for the most part. He didn't see me, I'm certain of that."

Dad stroked his chin. "And you don't think he was one of Willard's hired men?"

"No way."

Dad eyed me quizzically. "So what's your take?"

"I think he was from Acota. My guess is he works for Koffman."

"Good instincts, TJ."

"So what do we do?"

"Nothin' right now except tell Willard."

"That's gonna get him real hot and bothered," I said, concerned about Willard's hair-trigger temper.

"No doubt, but he needs to know what you saw just the same."

My dad's response sounded calculated, as if he'd thought the Acota problem through, sized up the risk to us and the valley as a whole, and pegged exactly how to tackle it. He leaned over and began gathering his tools and pump parts into a semicircle. When he had them neatly arranged in front of him, he said, "I learned somethin' I didn't know that might help the coalition legally when I was in Billings today meetin' with Ricky Peterson." He seemed in no rush whatsoever to share that information. "And by the way, Ricky said to tell you hello and that in spite of being tied to that big leather lawyer's chair of his most days, he can still out-fly-fish you."

I forced back a truncated sneeze. "No way," I said, but I wasn't really certain. Ricky had been right-handed before the fire at the seep. He'd had to relearn to fly-fish as a lefty. In fact, he'd had to relearn how to do pretty much everything. Jimmy's death soon after the fire had left him in a lingering funk until I'd been born, a latter-day replacement for his best friend. He was in his last year of college when he taught me to fly-fish. The sport became a steady source of our attachment and a reason for friendly competition until his law practice intervened.

I glanced around the dimly lit barn and found myself thinking about serendipity and coincidence and all the strange ghostly things that go bump in the night. Spoon's earlier admonition that there was a connection between the seep and my dad's trip to Billings threaded its way through my head. I couldn't fathom how Spoon could possibly have known about Ricky's accident at the gas seep. Looking puzzled, I asked, "Did you mention to Spoon that you were going into Billings to talk to Ricky?"

"No."

"Did Mom?"

"Pretty certain she didn't."

"Well, Spoon sure as heck knew you went, and I've got a feeling that he thinks there's a connection between that trespasser, Ricky, and our natural gas seep."

My dad shrugged. "What kinda connection?"

"Beats me," I said, noting that the pump was nearly assembled. "I just got a feeling, after talking to him about that rider and what I saw, that he can see something in all of this that you and I can't."

Dad chuckled. "Not another one of his premonitions."

Bats fluttered in the rafters as the barn door slid open, grating along on ancient wheels inside a concrete guide. Spoon stood in the open doorway. It had started to rain, and a thin mist filled the door opening. With the mist undulating behind him, Spoon somehow seemed suspended. "Got problems with the pump again?" he asked, closing the gap between us.

"Not for long," my dad said, standing and eyeing the reassembled pump. He looked at Spoon pensively, "Did Marva tell you I was goin' into Billings today?"

"Nope."

"Umm. Well, it sure as heck looks like I missed somethin' by traipsin' off to talk to Ricky Peterson instead of stickin' here. TJ told me about the trespassin' horseman. What's your take on what he mighta been up to?"

"Don't know exactly," Spoon said, glancing toward the rafters. "But I can tell you this. There's a connection between the rider TJ saw, your lawyer in Billings, and that old gas seep of yours. A connection that goes back to the root of our problems with Acota."

"Can you spell it out?" my dad asked, a note of disbelief in his tone.

"Nope. I just know there is one. What about your lawyer? Can you trust him?" Spoon asked with obvious reluctance.

"I damn sure can, regardless of any of your conjured-up visions." Dad shook his head, stepped over to the well, pump in hand, and began bolting the pump back into place. After securing two of the four bolts that held the pump to the well head, he looked up at Spoon, ratcheted down the final two bolts, and dusted off his hands. "You're way off base if you're thinkin' Ricky Peterson might be involved in any double-dealin' here, Spoon. Miles off."

"I didn't say he was," Spoon countered.

"Well, you damn sure implied it." Dad worked the pump handle up and down until he had a resistant vacuum. "No more prognosticatin' for now, okay?"

Spoon offered a reluctant "Okay" as a healthy stream of water poured from the pump's rusty spigot.

"Good. Now that that's settled and we got ourselves water, I say we pack it in for the evenin'." Dad dropped to one knee and began wiping down his tools with a moist shop rag. There was a clear tension between him and Spoon that I hadn't felt in a very long while—tension brought on by Spoon's soothsaying, the one thing about the hired man that my dad had never fully come to grips with, and the one thing that had the potential to pull them apart again.

Twelve

The following uneasy, muggy week was unseasonably hot. Each day the temperatures rose a notch until by week's end we were suffering through humid, windless days in the high eighties.

Spoon made a trip at the end of the week to the town of Colstrip, seventy-five miles north of our ranch, to search out the old Cheyenne Indian man who supposedly knew details about Elijah Witherspoon, the buffalo soldier who'd been killed in an avalanche a century earlier and who Spoon reasoned was his great-grandfather. He came home somber and empty-handed when the old man denied any knowledge of Elijah.

Disappointed, Spoon redoubled his efforts to search out his roots, taking on a schedule at the ranch that had him working from five to three and using the hours at the end of the workday to drive around the countryside and talk to people or go into Hardin to visit the library or courthouse and search through records before they closed.

On one of his days off, a day that was particularly overcast and gray, I watched him take off at six in the morning for parts unknown. When he came back that evening, looking tired and sullen, my mom asked him if he'd been able to track down any of his people. Looking forlorn, he walked past my mom and me as we picked grapes and mumbled, "Not really."

His churlish mood seemed to match that of my dad, who'd grown frustrated trying to coordinate a group of ranchers whose goals didn't quite mesh. A week after the shaky Willow Creek Ranchers Coalition was formed, word surfaced that the Demasters had not just leased their mineral rights to Acota, but were in the process of negotiating the sale of the entire ranch to the coal, oil, and gas barons, which meant Acota could potentially become not only an energy company exploring for minerals, but a cattle business competitor as well.

To add a lightning edge to things, a couple days after my sighting of the trespassing rider in gray, Willard Johnson had briefly spotted him near Four Corners, just down the hill from the natural gas seep. Neither my dad nor I had yet mentioned the trespasser to Willard. Dad hadn't had a chance to because of two trips he'd had to take to Billings—which made Willard boiling mad when he ultimately heard about the trespasser. When Dad finally broached the subject, Willard called Sheriff Woodson out to the ranch and had the sheriff ride the property with him on an old ATV. They looked for the rider in gray for hours with no luck. The next day Willard took to carrying an old Colt revolver and a 12-gauge shotgun with him.

A day later, when four men in a new red crew-cab truck with the Acota logo and an oil derrick inside a diamond stenciled on the front doors appeared near Four Corners, Willard took several shots at them.

The man behind the wheel, who happened to be the chief of Acota's coal exploration operations and a seasoned veteran of the agri-corporate energy wars, had encountered friction between ranchers and his company before, so Willard's shots didn't faze him. He simply pulled the vehicle into a protective stand of aspen and called Sheriff Woodson on his two-way. The sheriff in turn hastily called us out to Four Corners, along with Ed Koffman, Willard, Dale Turpin, and the Cundiffs.

Forty-five minutes later, Spoon, my dad, and I stood in a tight semicircle in the blazing noonday sun, fifteen feet from the brass survey pin that marked the spot where the four pioneer-family Willow Creek ranches came together. Ralph Cundiff, rocking nervously from side to side, and Willard Johnson stood just to my left. Dale Turpin stood next to Willard. With his right foot planted firmly on the survey marker, Sheriff Woodson stared stone faced at us from fifteen feet away. A few steps to the sheriff's right, Acota's field operations chief, who had been introduced by the sheriff as Larry Volks, stood rubbing his hands together. The three other men in the Acota truck had stayed in their vehicle, which was now parked just in front of the aspen stand. It was clear that their truck was on Willard's property and a good twenty yards west of our property line.

As we stood baking in the sun, trying to iron things out and waiting for Ed Koffman to arrive, I had the sense that had it been a hundred years earlier, given the same circumstances, someone might have been lying on the ground with a bullet in him.

Standing almost shoulder to shoulder, Spoon and my dad had barely moved since our arrival. It was as if any differences between them had evaporated the instant we'd taken off for Four Corners.

Spoon's eyes were locked on the horizon and the access road above us. The road, no more than a cow path, petered out just beyond the aspen stand and the Acota truck. Spoon had been reluctant to come along at first, but now, as he stood looking west, never altering his stance or his gaze, I sensed that we were moments away from someone or something appearing over the horizon.

When the clearly angry sheriff announced seconds after his walkie-talkie erupted in a blaze of static that Koffman was a minute or so away, I nodded to myself and whispered, "Knew it." I didn't like that Woodson looked somehow pleased over Koffman's impending arrival, nor did I like the fact that he kept gazing suspiciously toward Spoon, but under the circumstances, I knew better than to voice my opinions.

Spoon was the first to see dust rising in the distance. "Here he comes." He tipped his Stetson forward on his head and shaded his eyes with a cupped left hand.

"Don't see why we need a messiah from Acota playin' referee here," said Willard. "It's clear as a bell that Koffman's people were trespassin'." Willard glanced menacingly toward the Acota pickup and back at the sheriff. "I'm thinkin' you're a tad more partial to energy folks than us cattlemen, Cain, and I don't like it one bit."

"I'm not partial to anybody, damnit, Willard, and I'd appreciate it if you'd pipe down for a second. And for

the record, trespassin' or not, shootin' at someone consti-
tutes what the law generally views as unnecessary force,
maybe even assault." The sheriff glanced toward the calm-
looking Volks.

"Bullshit," said Willard, kicking at a huge anthill at
his feet. As thousands of ants scurried for cover, Willard
stomped after them, scowled at the sheriff, and reiterated,
"Bullshit."

Less than a minute later, a pickup identical in color,
make, and model to the one Willard had shot at rolled to
within fifty feet of us. I couldn't make out who the driver
was, but a serious Koffman began easing his way out of
the front passenger seat the instant the truck pulled to a
stop. Contrary to the image I'd conjured up during our
wait in the searing sun, Koffman didn't look either men-
acing or sleazy. Nor did he appear sly, calculating, or even
evil, as I'd heard him described by several members of the
coalition over the past week. What he looked like was a
jowly, determined, slightly less fidgety man than the one
who'd been at our house some eleven weeks earlier.

"Why the hell haven't you arrested Willard, Cain?"
Koffman called out, keeping his eyes locked on the sheriff
as he approached. "The man tried to shoot my field operations chief."

Koffman was on top of Woodson before the other man
could respond, wagging an index finger at him and kicking
the dirt. "He's a reactionary fool!" Koffman bellowed, obviously intent on putting on a show. The only reaction he got
from Willard, however, was an unresponsive stare generated
by my dad's raised-eyebrow plea for Willard to cool it.

When I looked at Spoon to gauge his reaction, I realized that his gaze was fixed on the man who'd driven Koffman to the scene and who now stood stoically next to the crew cab's open driver's-side door.

Spoon's eyes never moved from the driver—and suddenly, neither did mine. Standing there, six foot two at least, as broad shouldered and muscular as my dad, was the trespassing horseman, outfitted from head to toe in gray. He was wearing expensive lizard-skin boots, and his shirt and gabardine pants looked as if they'd been tailored. Except for the absence of his Johnny Reb cap and the diamond earring in his left earlobe, something I hadn't been able to see from a distance the day I'd first spotted him, he was the magnified image of the man I'd seen exploring our natural gas seep. His aquamarine eyes were mesmerizing, and his nearly shoulder-length hair, a little longer than Spoon's, gave him a ghostly George Armstrong Custer look.

My jaw dropped, and I muttered, "Damn." When I glanced over at Spoon and my dad, whose eyes were also set on the man in gray, I swore I saw a hint of recognition in Spoon's eyes. As I stood gawking, looking back and forth between the three men, I realized that Spoon was dissecting our trespasser. When the man looked past me and directly at Spoon as he walked over to join Koffman, I had the sense that he was just as intently examining Spoon. It seemed that the strange evaluative process would continue indefinitely until Ed Koffman broke the silence.

"Can we get this over with, Cain? I don't have all day to stand out here in the sun and bake." As if he needed to add something more profound, Koffman said to no one in particular, "We may be the unwanted and the unwelcomed out here right now, gentlemen, but trust me, in the end we'll have our way."

My dad bristled as Willard Johnson, unable to control himself any longer, shouted, "The hell you will!"

Looking pleased that he'd finally ruffled Willard, Koffman said, "The Demasters have folded their tent, in case you missed it, Willard. Others will follow." There was a grating smugness in his tone.

"You fuckin'..." Willard reared back, lowered his head, and charged the startled-looking Koffman.

Sheriff Woodson took a step forward to shove Willard aside, but the man in gray was quicker, and the short, swift karate chop he landed just beneath the back of Willard's skull sent him sprawling.

"Damnit!" The sheriff unholstered his 9-millimeter, raised it skyward, and squeezed off two rounds. The crack of gunfire froze everyone, including the man in gray, and my dad and Spoon squatted in preparation for rushing the mysterious trespasser. "I'll use this thing!" Woodson stepped back to help the dazed Willard get up.

As Willard stumbled to his feet, the sheriff eyed the man in gray. "Now, friend, just who the hell are you?"

It was Ed Koffman who responded. "He's Matt Rodue, chief of field operations security at Acota."

"Pretty quick to react, aren't we, Mr. Rodue?" said the sheriff, holstering his weapon.

Rodue remained silent as the thoroughly embarrassed Willard Johnson dusted himself off.

Looking incensed, the sheriff said, "Well, Mr. Rodue, since you seem bent on swallowin' your tongue, here's a two-word note for you to tack up on your office wall back at corporate headquarters. *No trespassin'!* Your people were trespassin' on private property, friend, and out here that's a no-no. You got it?"

"They lost their bearings, Cain," said Koffman, again running interference. "Four huge ranches coming together at this one spot. It's easy to get turned around."

"Easy, smeasy—your folks were on land they don't belong on," said the sheriff. "Do it again and I'll get an injunction to keep your vehicles out of the whole damn county. Your buddies over there by the aspen, quakin' in their boots inside their truck, damn near started a war."

The sheriff stared us down one by one. "So here, my good folks, is the skinny. Bill, I want you and that ex-con hired man of yours to stay inside your fences. Willard—I need you to do the same. And while you're at it, for God's sake, try and check your temper. The same goes for the rest of you," he said, eyeing Dale Turpin and finally Ralph Cundiff, who'd both been strangely silent.

Turning to face Koffman, he said, "As for you, Ed, and your karate-kid friend here, stay the hell off private property. Am I clear?"

Sounding neither acquiescent nor sincere, Koffman said, "Yes."

His voice still booming, the sheriff said, "I'm gonna be forced to file a long, detailed report about what happened here today, and that's gonna take me away from things I should be doin' that are more important. I don't ever wanna have to file another such report about problems out here in this valley for as long as I'm sheriff, because if I do, somebody's gonna pay. Now, I want everybody here to get back on the horse, wagon, truck, ATV, or whatever the hell they rode in on and disperse."

Koffman offered a meek okay as we all moved to leave. When I glanced at Spoon, I realized he was seething. As he, my dad, and I walked toward our pickup, Spoon said, "Woodson's an ass."

He turned back to stare at where we'd all been standing, locking his gaze not on the sheriff but on Matt Rodue, who was down on one knee examining the Four Corners pin.

When Rodue looked up to return Spoon's gaze, Spoon said, "Your man in gray is stream poison, TJ." He flashed my dad a look that as much as said, *You'll see.*

As the three of us continued to stare at him, Rodue rose and headed back toward the pickup he'd driven in. As he walked toward the vehicle with his back toward us, I could have sworn I heard him snicker.

Thirteen

There wasn't much to the rest of the afternoon except lingering heat and the feeling, as I rehashed the day's events over and over in my head, that the confrontation at Four Corners was just the start of things to come.

Spoon and I finished some overdue equipment maintenance in our machine shop. My dad made a couple of lengthy calls to Ricky Peterson, and mom assembled and washed her canning paraphernalia.

A little past four, Dad asked me to go into Hardin to pick up a couple of culverts he'd ordered for a windmill access road that had a tendency to wash out during early fall snows. We were standing by a flowering crab apple tree in our front yard, a tree he'd planted the year I'd been born that for some reason always bloomed much later than its neighbors. As I fumbled with the keys to my pickup, I noticed that a cluster of leaves near the top had already turned bright orange.

"Late starter, early finisher," my dad said, noting the intensity in my face. "You decided about school?"

I'd thought long and hard about heading off to Missoula and the University of Montana in January, but I hadn't exactly decided to go yet. Although the ranch was running as efficiently as it had in years, we'd had a good hay crop, and our calves were fat and as fall-market ready as I'd ever seen, I had the feeling that if I left, Willow Creek would somehow flounder. "I'm still mulling it over," I finally said.

"Have you told your mom that?" he asked, clearly surprised. "You know she and I are on the same page about you and school."

"Nope. Haven't said anything to Spoon either."

"I'd let 'em both know real soon, if I were you. I'd hate to be on the wrong side of her wishes. As for Spoon, he's got a right to know if he's gonna have to bear a bigger share of the load."

"I will," I said, suspecting that his remarks were merely perfunctory and that he was wrestling with issues a lot more serious than my going off to college.

"Good." He massaged one temple as if he was some how shifting the gears in his head. "Spoon really stared that Rodue fella down, didn't he? Wonder if he knows something we don't."

"Got a feeling Spoon saw something in Rodue that we couldn't."

"My take too," he said, adjusting his belt. "I've asked Ricky Peterson to do a little checkin' up on Rodue while he's tryin' to figure out how the coalition should deal with Koffman and Acota. I've got a feelin' Rodue knows about as much about runnin' security for an energy exploration company as I do. My bet would be that Rodue's no more than hired muscle."

"Safe bet. Especially seeing how he went after Willard."

"I'm hopin' he took his aggressions back to Billings

and Acota headquarters with him, but in case he didn't, keep an eye out for him when you're out workin'. I'll let Spoon and your mom know to do the same."

"Mom?" I asked with surprise.

"Absolutely. She's another set of eyes, and havin' another set of eyes focused on a problem never hurts. Besides, I've seen her shoot the head off more than a few rattlesnakes with that .410 of hers." Dad smiled. "Your mom has never taken kindly to having snakes in her midst."

"She wouldn't shoot Rodue," I said, chuckling and turning to head for my pickup.

Dad's response was both chilling and matter of fact. "She would if she had to, son."

I knew he was right.

Deadpan, Dad said, "All's fair in love and war, TJ, and since we've had ourselves a hostile action out here in our valley, I'd say we're on the cusp of our own little war. Now, hurry on into town and get those culverts before Ranchers and Farmers United closes."

I sprinted for my pickup and quickly headed down the half-mile gravel lane that led from our house. It was lined on both sides by a five-rail fence made of four-inch-diameter oil rigger's pipe. I'd seen cattle trailers bounce off that fence and leave barely a dent in it, and I'd heard my mom say more than once after a truck loaded with steers had drifted off the road and into the fence that the problem was just about always with the driver and rarely with the truck. "People," she was fond of saying, "have a hard time keeping on the straight and narrow." As I watched our house disappear in the rearview mirror, I couldn't help but think about my dad's comments about her and smile. There was no question that she could handle a .410 better than either of us, and none whatsoever that, armed with one, she was pure death to rattlesnakes.

I waved at Spoon as I rolled slowly past the machine shop, where he stood in the doorway toweling off his hands. I wondered as I bumped toward the highway what kind of darkness he'd seen in Matt Rodue. I reminded myself to ask him as soon as I got back home.

◢ ◢ ◢

Hardin seemed sleepier than normal when I arrived twenty-five minutes later. I suspected that most people in town were hiding from the unseasonable heat. As I waited at a stop sign at the intersection of Center Avenue and Third and watched the time and temperature display on the First Interstate Bank flash eighty-eight degrees, I found myself wondering whether twenty years down the road I'd still be riding into Hardin for supplies in a pickup with ninety-five thousand miles on it. If I'd still be breaking Willow Creek ice in the middle of the winter to open up a watering hole for livestock; if my mother and father would still be alive; if Spoon would still be around; and even if we'd still own the ranch.

Even if I finished college and went on to vet school, as my mom had always wanted, I suspected that, like my dad, I'd always be shackled to the land. Although in most ways that wouldn't be bad, I knew there was more to the world than the fourteen thousand acres of Willow Creek Ranch, or Hardin, or even Montana.

My wanderlust had only surfaced in the past year, and it had more to do with listening to Spoon than anything else. I'd listened to him talk about where he'd been and where he was going, drinking in his travel tales and wishing they were my own. As near as I could determine, Spoon had been in nearly every state in the Union. He'd picked apples in Washington State, worked in a steel mill in Pittsburgh, and farmed in Indiana, Ohio, and Kentucky. He'd broken horses in New Mexico, repaired bridges in the Mississippi Delta, and hauled trash on Cape Cod in Massachusetts.

On those occasions when he'd had a drink or two to bolster his tales, a sadness deep inside him bubbled to the surface, and he'd end up telling stories about the 50-caliber machine gun he'd manned on the aft deck of the navy patrol boat he'd served on during Vietnam. A gun he'd affectionately called Bertha.

Spoon had been to places and seen things I could only dream of, and of late I'd begun to imagine seeing those places too. The ranch, as far as I was concerned, would always be there, massive, imposing, peaceful, and sometimes even tragic. Although I'd often wondered how I would keep it going if it ever became my responsibility, I'd never questioned whether I could.

There was only one other vehicle, a longbed dually pickup, parked in the narrow, rectangular parking lot of Ranchers and Farmers United Feed Supply when I pulled in. One of the store's clerks, a man I knew only as Swenson, was straining to help a customer load a generator into the truck bed. I watched Swenson, perspiring and cursing, struggle with the generator as I got out of my vehicle and headed for the store. The air-conditioning inside beat the hell out of the weak, intermittent AC in my truck, a unit my dad had been promising to repair all summer. I was enjoying the newfound comfort until I realized that the only other person in the store was Becky Walterman, the daughter of the store's owner, likely home for a long weekend from the University of Wyoming. A lump filled my throat.

Becky and I had dated during the last two years of high school, committed to one another with the kind of bond that only first love can generate. When she'd gone off to Laramie following graduation and I'd stayed at the ranch, the bond had stretched and ultimately broken. I'd seen her only a few times since we'd amicably called it quits, and I'd had the sense that while I was marking time, Becky was moving forward.

I walked slowly toward Becky and the store's ten-foot-long maple masterpiece of a checkout counter, which had been nicked, gouged, and smoothed to its golden tan patina by more than seventy years' worth of use. I was hoping to find the right words to say when Becky called out cheerfully, "TJ, I bet you're here for those culverts."

"Sure am," I said, thankful that she'd spoken first.

"They're sitting out by the loading-dock doors. I'll cash you out and get Swenson to help you load them up." She smiled, scooted into the cramped space behind the counter, and eased her supple competitive-swimmer's body behind the antique cash register. I couldn't help but notice how beautiful she looked. A deep summer tan highlighted her hazel-gray eyes, and her stylish, jet-black hair, shorter than I remembered her wearing it, glimmered. She'd always been a head shorter than I, but somehow, as she stood smiling behind the cash register, she seemed taller.

I reminded myself that, even dressed in faded jeans and an untucked old work shirt, I was still the lean, athletic, six-foot-two, all-state high school basketball star I'd once been. "It's gonna be a charge," I said.

Becky looked disappointed, as if she'd been prepared to ring up a cash sale on the register and signal once and for all that we were done. "Hear you're headed for Missoula in January." Retrieving the tally book her dad reserved for his long-term customers' charges, she pulled out a charge slip. Seeing the surprised look on my face, she offered a disclaimer. "Heard it from Harriet Rankin. She's sorta sweet on that hired man of yours, you know."

"No, I didn't know."

"Well, put on your glasses, TJ. I've seen the two of 'em eating here in town at the Merry Mixer restaurant twice."

Thinking I needed to defend Spoon in order to protect him from being hurt in the same way I had been, I said, "She's helping him search out his family roots."

Looking unconvinced, Becky said, "I see." She totaled up the bill and slid the charge slip my way.

"How'd you like your first year at Wyoming?" I asked, hoping to take the edge off what had become a difficult conversation.

"Loved it. Made the swim team and the dean's list."

That wasn't exactly what I wanted to hear. I wanted to hear about the college boy who'd beaten me out. I wanted to know what was so special about him, what he did for her that I didn't, couldn't, or hadn't been able to do. But instead of asking, I methodically folded the charge slip into thirds and slipped it into my shirt pocket. "Hope you have a great sophomore year."

"I'm looking forward to it. And I know you'll knock 'em dead up at the U of M in January."

I thought I saw a flash of parting sadness cross Becky's face as I turned to leave. Perhaps it was simply a look of pity. "I'll do my best," I said, heading for the loading dock.

Minutes later, Swenson stood next to the skidster he'd used to load the two culverts into my pickup. Sun rays twinkled off the culverts' galvanized metal, punctuating the fact that Mother Nature was still in charge of the thermometer. "Hot enough for you?" Swenson asked, removing his cap and wiping his brow.

"Sure is."

"How are your ma and pa?"

"Fine."

"Well, tell 'em I said howdy, and be sure and crank up the air in that truck of yours on the way home." Slipping his cap back on, Swenson jumped into the skidster, grabbed a half-finished Coke off the seat, took a swig, and headed toward a shed near the back of the property.

As I stood there sweating and wondering what it would be like to load farm and ranch supplies all day long for the rest of my life, I decided that what I needed to prepare me for the uncomfortable ride home was something that would take my mind off Becky and all the wouldas and couldas I'd probably conjure up on the drive back to the ranch. A trip to Dandy Tom's Sundry Shop and a vanilla malt seemed just about right.

Dandy Tom's, four blocks due north of the Ranchers and Farmers United, was a place I'd frequented since before grade school. The place sold the best rock candy and malts I'd ever tasted. As I parked diagonally in front of the store, thinking about everything from ice cream to cows and what exactly college life might be like, a pickup pulled into the neighboring spot on my driver's side. I didn't notice the Acota logo on the door until I was nearly out of my vehicle. When Ed Koffman eased his considerable bulk out of the other truck, we nearly bumped shoulders. "Young Mr. Darley," he said, uttering my name as if he were introducing me to someone.

The driver's-side door opened seconds later, and the expressionless Matt Rodue stepped out. Dressed in his customary gray, he sported aviator sunglasses. To my surprise, he clutched a black Stetson in his right hand instead of his Johnny Reb cap.

Koffman broke into a broad, toothy grin. "Thought I saw one of your daddy's pickups down at Ranchers and Farmers United." He glanced toward the front door of Dandy Tom's. "Got yourself a sweet tooth, I see."

I wanted to tell him that the pickup I was driving was mine and that I'd paid for it on my own, but I thought better of it. "Figured I'd enjoy a malt on the ride home," I said, heading for Dandy Tom's.

Koffman nodded understandingly. "Good medicine on a scorcher like this."

I'd reached the sidewalk when Koffman caught up with me. He sounded almost breathless. "You know, you're heir to an awful lot of land out there at Willow Creek, TJ, and every acre's worth its weight in gold. I've talked to your folks about securing your future, but frankly I haven't gotten very far. Thought I'd talk to you on my own. Mainly because I'm not quite certain how much you share their enthusiasm for ranching."

I glanced at Rodue, who'd begun to impatiently twirl his Stetson in his hand, then back at Koffman. All of a sudden a granny gear somewhere deep inside me overrode all my manners. "Take a hike, Koffman. And take your fucking trained ape with you."

"Tsk, tsk, tsk, TJ. I wouldn't resort to cursing and name-calling if I were you. Orneriness doesn't become you. Your mom would be disappointed, surely."

I don't know where the courage I summoned up came from, or if what I saw as courage wasn't simply foolhardiness. Wagging an index finger in Koffman's face before tapping him twice in the chest, I said, "You won't ever move a grain of dirt on our land. Much less any coal. Not now, not ever, and if—"

Rodue grabbed my left hand and bent it backward until I choked out a painful "Oomph."

"You're an arrogant smart-ass, son, and an imprudent one at that," said Koffman. He waved Rodue off, but Rodue refused to let go. He inched my hand backward as I tried not to scream.

I was at the painful point of screaming "Please let go!" when a voice called out from a pickup that had pulled up next to us. "Let go of the boy's hand, Rodue."

I looked toward the street to see Spoon behind the wheel. He was leaning across the front seat and toward the open passenger window. The barrel of 20-gauge shotgun poked from the window, aimed not at Rodue, but directly at Koffman.

My fingers had gone numb when, responding to a nod from Koffman, Rodue finally let go.

"Good show," Spoon called out as another pickup, its driver oblivious to what was happening, rolled by.

As the nose of the 20-gauge disappeared, the suddenly twitching Koffman said, "Same to you, Mr. Witherspoon. That is, if you're into either bluffing or theatrics. Just remember this, though," he added, glancing at Rodue. "We never bluff."

Ignoring Koffman, Spoon said, "Get in your truck, TJ, and I'll trail ya home."

Rubbing my hand in an attempt to restore the circulation, I ran to my pickup. As I slipped the truck into gear, Spoon called out in as piercing and determined a voice as I had ever heard from him, "Neither do I, asshole. Neither do I."

Fourteen

I continued to shake like someone with the DTs until Spoon and I had descended into the Willow Creek valley. A few minutes later, as we made our way down the ranch lane and home, I noticed a car parked near our house that I didn't recognize. When I rolled down my window to get a better look, Ricky Peterson waved at me from our front yard, where he and my dad stood talking. Only then did I realize that the late-model BMW was his. "Talk to you later," Ricky yelled as Spoon and I drove by. He and dad turned and walked toward the house.

Spoon wouldn't tell me why he'd followed me into town or how he could possibly have known that Koffman and Rodue would be there to greet me as I left. As we walked toward the tack room and bunkhouse, I peppered him with questions. When I pressed him to tell me how on earth he'd known where I'd be in Hardin, or that I'd be in trouble, he simply said, "A mother cow knows when she's got a calf with a problem, TJ."

Why we didn't go straight to my dad and tell him what had happened in town, I can't say. Maybe it had to do with me not wanting to run to him for help like some schoolboy. I can't speak for Spoon, but for the longest time afterward I rationalized that his silence had something to do with Ricky Peterson's being there. Deep down, however, I knew our silence had more to do with the bond between Spoon and me: a strange blood-brothers kind of connection that had caused him to follow me into Hardin in the first place and save me from both embarrassment and harm.

As I looked around Spoon's cramped but comfortably appointed quarters, I realized that he'd made use of nearly every one of the old saddle blankets and rugs that had been in the tack room on the day of his arrival. Weavings were draped over sawhorses, and several more rugs had been framed and hung to the walls. The rugs and saddle blankets had been mended, rewoven, or patched so that not a moth hole, tear, or corner of an unraveled edge remained visible.

"When'd you set out all the blankets and rugs?" I asked, certain they hadn't all been on display the last time I'd visited.

"A couple of days ago," Spoon said, beaming. "Can't see the flaws, can ya? Got Harriet to thank for that. She's quite the reweaver and seamstress."

"She sure is," I said, examining one of the rugs. "Heard about the two of you hanging out in Hardin," I added with a teasing grin.

The smile on Spoon's face disappeared. "Then I expect you ain't heard the truth."

"Sorry," I said, embarrassed.

"No need to be. Just never been real big on havin' what's private between two people fanned by rumors." The look on Spoon's face softened. "Now, why don't you tell me what it was you said to Koffman and Rodue that caused you to end up in that Chinese hand clasp."

"I sorta told Koffman to shove off after he rubbed me the wrong way. Nudged him a little, too, but only with one finger."

Spoon laughed. "Sounds to me like you disturbed the man's space. It's a wonder he didn't call the sheriff on the spot and charge you with assault."

"When all's said and done, he might. After all, you did point a shotgun at him."

"And I'da used it if I had to."

"Think we should tell my dad?"

"Soon enough," said Spoon. "I'm thinkin' that right now he's got enough on his plate. No need loadin' him down no more."

"Okay, but you know how he and my mom hate being left out of the loop."

"They'll be inside the whole wide-arcin' circle soon enough, and so will that Rodue fellow and Koffman." Spoon's tone had an ominous air of certainty that briefly unsettled me.

"Rodue sure drifted in outta the blue. Where do you think he came from?"

"Don't know," Spoon said, kneeling and inspecting one of the rugs on the floor. "But I've got Harriet checkin' up on him." He tugged at the edge of the rug. "I'm sure she'll do her usual thorough job."

We talked a while longer. Not about Rodue or the fact that Rodue now had both Ricky Peterson and Harriet investigating him, or even about ranching or coalitions, but about where I saw myself going in life. When I told Spoon I wasn't certain about the direction I'd take, he chuckled and said, "It'll find you when you're out there on a ledge all by your lonesome. An upslope wind usually does."

△ △ △

I left Spoon's quarters that evening confused and a little hurt. He seemed to have Harriet in his corner, if not under his thumb, yet he wouldn't admit to me that there was anything romantic between them. But I'd never mentioned Becky Walterman to him either, so in a sense we were even. And although he seemed certain that Koffman and Rodue would resurface, he'd been reluctant to offer any specifics about where and when. I felt even more ill at ease after Ricky Peterson and my dad, looking as nervous as expectant fathers, gave me less than two minutes of their time in what amounted to a dismissive pat on the head when I ran into them on my way back to the house.

As I stood in the ebbing twilight and watched them chat in low whispers as they headed for Ricky's car, I felt petty and unincluded. That feeling of isolation stayed with me for the rest of the night as I wrestled with the fact that I hadn't told my father, mother, or Ricky about what had happened in Hardin.

△ △ △

The next morning at a few minutes past ten, Sylvester King, our rural-route mailman of more than twenty years, a bug-eyed, stick-figured Ichabod Crane of a man given to runny noses and hysteria, stood pounding on our front door screaming at the top of his lungs that he'd just found Willard Johnson dead. He'd discovered Willard lying in a hay meadow near his house next to his overturned John Deere 8760 tractor. Willard's skull had been crushed.

Sylvester had had the good sense to call 911 on his two-way before rushing the two miles from where he'd found Willard to our house. By the time he'd given the news to my mom, the only one home at the time, upsetting her normal rock steadiness with his out-of-breath gesticulations and guttural pleas for help, he was sweating like a racehorse. She left him standing on our front porch, shaking, drinking a glass of ice water, and perspiring, and rounded up Spoon and me from the machine shop, where we were busy fabricating stabilizing footings for the two culverts we planned to set that day. The three of us immediately headed out in one of our pickups for our south horse pasture to collect my dad.

We spotted him several minutes later, kneeling next to his horse, Smokey. Smokey was holding a hoof off the ground as my dad massaged his left hind fetlock.

"Don't rile him," he called out as Spoon brought the pickup to a stop several yards away and the three of us got out. "Poor guy stepped in a gopher hole, and he's gone a little lame."

I hoped that the injury to the amazingly spry nineteen-year-old horse my dad had raised from a colt was minor. Born nine months before me, and the calmest, most steady and most majestic horse I'd ever run across, Smokey had helped my dad transition through the dark days after Jimmy's death.

Dad shook his head and ran his hand from fetlock to hock. "Nineteen years of runnin' all over this place, not one day of sickness, and he goes and steps in a gopher hole."

Hesitant to serve up another problem and in as calm a voice as she could muster, my mom said, "There's been a terrible accident, Bill. Willard Johnson's dead. Sylvester King found him a little while ago with his skull crushed in, lying next to that new tractor he bought this spring. It was overturned."

"Shit!" The fact that my dad had cursed, and in front of my mom, caused me a start. "Been expectin' trouble, but nothin' like this," he said. The look he flashed Spoon told me that he'd more than likely been mulling over Spoon's prediction of trouble for weeks. "Let me see how well Smokey can walk and we'll head on over to Willard's." He rose, grabbed the big bay's reins, and led him in a tight half circle. "Come on, Smoke. Show me what you're made of, boy." Smokey hobbled every step of the way.

"Don't think he can make it," Dad said to Spoon. "Better go get a horse trailer. We're gonna have to haul him back home."

As Spoon turned to leave, my dad called after him, "And Spoon, make sure the trailer you bring has a horse-doctorin' kit."

Spoon sprinted back to the pickup, wheeled the truck around, and was headed back to headquarters when mom asked, "You don't think Willard's death had anything to do with those Acota people or Koffman, do you, Bill?"

"Don't really know," Dad said, running an open hand reassuringly along Smokey's withers. "Maybe we should've asked Spoon." He cupped a hand to his eyes and watched the rooster tail of dust rise from behind Spoon's pickup. "He's the one in the crystal-ball business."

△ △ △

By the time my folks and I reached what my mom insisted on calling *the accident site*, Sheriff Woodson and one of his deputies were on the scene. Spoon had stayed behind to watch Smokey and wait for the vet. The sheriff had cordoned off a twenty-five-by-twenty-five-foot area around Willard's overturned tractor and was busy examining one of the tractor's rear tires. A few feet from the tractor, a tarpaulin covered Willard's body. All that was visible at one edge were the soles of Willard's run-over work boots. Sylvester King, nervous and still shaking, stood between the sheriff and the three of us.

"Hell of a heavy piece of equipment to flip over out here in the middle of a perfectly level hay field," said Woodson, leaning against the tractor tire, stroking his chin, and aiming the comment at no one in particular. "Stranger still that old Willard, a man with tens of thousands of hours behind the wheel of a tractor, would turn one on its side. Wouldn't you agree, Bill?"

"Pretty much."

The sheriff glanced down at the tarp. "I'd say it would be a real uncommon circumstance for old Willard to have hit his head on the one oversized, razor-sharp rock that happened to be jutting up outta this meadow as well. Could be coincidence, I guess," he said with a noncommittal shrug. "How'd you happen to be down here and find him, Sylvester?"

"He had a certified piece of mail I needed his signature on."

"Good thing he did or we might notta found him for days."

The sheriff's matter-of-fact tone upset my mom. "He's got kin in Great Falls and other folks who cared about him, Harvey. How about a touch of humanity on your part?" she said with displeasure.

"Yeah, I know." Woodson looked only slightly and briefly embarrassed. "I wouldn't want to think that Willard's meetin' his maker had anything to do with any of the problems you folks out here in the Willow Creek valley are havin' with Acota Energy. There's been enough pushin', shovin', and name-callin' already. Wouldn't want to think it escalated to this." He eyed the tarp and shook his head.

"We didn't start the pushin' or the shovin'," my dad shot back.

The sheriff turned and looked directly at me. "Maybe not, but from what I hear from Ed Koffman, you're keeping it going. He charged into the office yesterday and complained that TJ assaulted him. To make matters worse, he said that hired man of yours, Witherspoon, threatened him with a shotgun. I was plannin' on comin' by your place to discuss the issue today. Didn't expect I'd have to deal with a bigger problem."

"What's he talkin' about, TJ?" my dad asked.

Knowing there was no way to sugarcoat what had happened, I said, with as much self-assurance as I could muster, "Koffman and that wingman of his, Rodue, and I had a little stand-off in town yesterday."

"Why didn't you tell me about it?" There was clear disappointment and more than a hint of harshness in my dad's tone.

When my mom, looking and sounding astonished, said, "Why didn't you, TJ?" I wanted to sink into the ground.

"I thought it was pretty minor."

"There's nothin' minor about pullin' a shotgun on someone, son," said Woodson.

"Spoon had to. Otherwise Rodue would've broken my wrist."

"What in God's name?" my mom said in as loud a voice as I suspected she'd used in years.

The sheriff shook his head. "Like I said, we're all gonna need to talk. Tell you this up front, though. I don't like the idea of an ex-con levelin' a shotgun on folks I'm sworn to protect. Don't like it one bit."

"Did Koffman file a complaint?" my dad asked.

"No."

"Well, then. There's two sides to every coin. I'm guessin' Koffman would've pushed a whole lot harder if he figured he was gonna come up a clear winner on the issue. You got no complaint, you got no case, as far as I'm concerned."

"Unless you're dealin' with an ex-con," the sheriff shot back. Agitated and trying to restore some sense of order to things, he said, "We'll talk later, Bill. Right now I've got a possible homicide on my hands."

Dusting off his hands as if to punctuate the point, Woodson turned, as we all suddenly did, in the direction of an approaching vehicle. "That'll be my crime-scene technician," he said. "And that means I've got work to do. I'm gonna have to ask everyone to leave."

Dad nodded and said, "Okay. When you're ready to talk about what happened in Hardin yesterday, come on by the ranch." His words were meant for the sheriff, but all the while he was looking at me. "I'll be at home all day, and so will TJ."

"Want to make sure that hired man of yours, Witherspoon, is around too?"

"Oh, he'll be around. Count on it."

As we moved to leave, my dad took one last look at Willard Johnson's remains. He didn't say anything. He simply frowned and shook his head.

△ △ △

The trip back to the ranch was tense and pretty much silent. Not a word was spoken until we headed up the lane to the house.

"Round up Spoon, would you?" Dad said to me tersely, "And meet me on the front porch in five minutes."

It seemed to me afterward that I was out of the truck before it had actually stopped. I found Spoon in the barn tending to Smokey. The horse's injured hind leg was wrapped with a support bandage almost up to the hock.

"He's doin' great," Spoon said, turning to me as he stroked Smokey's neck. "Doc Williams sedated him.

Nothin' but a sprain. Like your pa said, he'll be fine."

Swallowing hard, I said, "We're sure not."

Spoon looked puzzled. "Somethin' else serious turn up over at Johnson's?"

"Yeah. My dad found out about our run-in with Koffman and Rodue from Sheriff Woodson. Woodson's planning on paying us a visit later today. Said he wants to talk to you in particular."

"Then I'm thinkin' maybe we should roll out the red carpet for him." Spoon patted Smokey's hock and chuckled.

"It's no joking matter, Spoon. My dad's pissed as hell over me not telling him about what happened, and the sheriff sounds about ready to bring his ex-con hammer down on your head."

"Then let him," Spoon said defiantly.

At a loss for words and uncertain what to do next, I said, "Dad's tapping his foot out on the front porch."

Spoon stroked Smokey gently behind the left ear, and said, "You'll be all right, big fellow. You're just outta the game for a couple of innings."

Glancing at me, he said, "Lead the way, TJ. Might as well get this over with." When he closed the gate to Smokey's stall behind him and we headed for the house, I had the sense that a gate might have closed between the two of us as well.

△ △ △

My dad was a man who generally saw things in terms of right or wrong. As he stood on our porch and listened to Spoon's description of what had happened in Hardin the previous afternoon, I could tell that he was having a difficult time assessing who had been in the wrong. To his way of thinking, if you leveled a weapon at any living creature—man, woman, or beast—you were expected to use it or suffer the consequences. By the same token, in his world, if you chose to pick on someone smaller or weaker than you and they somehow served you your comeuppance, it was probably well deserved. It was only when Spoon said, "Rodue woulda broken TJ's wrist and enjoyed the sounds of the bones poppin'," that I saw a hint of anger in his eyes.

Looking me squarely in the eye, he asked, "Think Rodue would've snapped your wrist if Spoon hadn't showed up?"

"No question."

My dad stroked his chin thoughtfully. "And what would you have done if he had, Spoon?"

"Woulda had no choice but to shoot the man," Spoon said calmly.

There was a stretch of silence as the three of us stood there looking at one another and breathing noticeably. When my dad finally said, "Afraid I would've shot him too," I knew that for him the issue was settled. "Wouldn't have wanted to, but I woulda done it."

When he turned back to face me, the look on his face said, *Let's move on.*

We did so quickly. Eyeing both of us, Dad asked, "So now that we've dealt with one issue, at least in terms of me having a fuller understandin' of what occurred in town yesterday, what's your take on Willard Johnson's death? Think maybe Koffman or Rodue might've helped old Willard up the stairs a little early?"

Spoon's answer caught him off guard. "Don't really know. No question they mighta had thousands of acres of coal reserves and millions of dollars' worth of reasons to kill the man, but I wouldn't be so quick to label 'em murderers. Coulda been just another freak farmin' accident."

"Guess it could've," my dad said, still pressing. "No feelin' in your gut about what might've happened one way or the other?"

"Nope."

Dad looked disappointed. The one time it seemed to matter most, and the one time he wanted to draw on Spoon's purported clairvoyance, Spoon hadn't come through. "Too bad," he said, shaking his head, "because once word about Willard's death gets out, some folks in this valley are gonna push long and hard against any point of view that says his death was accidental."

"Afraid you're right," said Spoon. "Just hope they recognize that a lot of times when you think long, you think wrong."

"I'll advise folks of that when Ricky Peterson meets with the coalition tomorrow evenin'. But I've got a feelin' it may well fall on deaf ears."

Fifteen

Few people in the valley disputed the Big Horn County coroner's autopsy findings, which stated that Willard Johnson had died from a fractured skull. And some even accepted the story line supporting the possibility that the knife-edged rock that had been the death instrument could have found its way into the middle of an otherwise rockless hay meadow as the result of happenstance. Almost no one, however, was giving credence to Sheriff Woodson's testimony, offered at a hastily called inquest, of his belief that Willard Johnson's death was unequivocally accidental. No assemblage of photographs showing twenty-foot drag marks in the dirt, or pictures of the fresh dirt trapped beneath Willard's fingernails, suggesting that he'd tried to crawl for help after accidentally tipping his tractor over and hitting his head, could sway the issue.

Aside from my parents, most people were convinced that Willard's death had been orchestrated by Ed Koffman, his field security chief, Matt Rodue, and the corporate thugs at Acota Energy. Initially my dad pressed hard to convince coalition members to keep an open mind on the issue, but as the days passed, his attempts became less hardy. Angry, distrustful, and fearful, several ranchers in the valley had taken to wearing sidearms, and as a result of the tension, the coalition was slowly disintegrating.

The Demasters, harassed and threatened by several coalition members for selling out to Acota in the first place, had had two mysterious fires start on their property over a span of three weeks. The fires charred close to thirty acres each before they could be put out.

The Demasters claimed that Dale Turpin had started the fires as retribution. Angry to the point of cursing out Rulon Demaster one day in front of Lammer's Trading Post in Hardin and threatening legal action for defamation, Turpin denounced the Demasters as pompous, privileged outsiders who'd never been welcome in our valley in the first place, suggesting before stomping off that the sooner they left, the better.

The dissension in coalition ranks escalated even further when word spread that Willard Johnson's niece and the lone heir to his estate, Thelma Lawson, a fifth-grade teacher from Great Falls, and her husband, Jarvon, a wimpish, hard-of-hearing electrician, were planning on keeping the ranch but leasing all of the mineral rights to Acota.

Although Ralph and Maxine Cundiff remained, at least on the surface, true to the cause, my dad confessed to my mom at breakfast the day after the news about Thelma Lawson's intentions had leaked out that he wouldn't be surprised to see the Cundiffs eventually cave in as well.

Only Dale Turpin held the line as steadfastly as us, repeatedly emphasizing at coalition meetings that before he leased out his coal rights, he'd rot in hell. There was a downside to Turpin's stalwartness, however—at least for us. His ranch didn't actually meet ours except at Four Corners, and like us, for the most part he bordered the

Demaster's land. I'd heard Ricky Peterson tell my dad during one of his increasingly frequent visits that even if Turpin held strong to his convictions, his Quarter Circle V Ranch and our Willow Creek Ranch could end up looking like two weights at the end of a barbell, connected by a narrow, strip-mined, two-mile spit of intervening Demaster land.

When Ricky appeared at the ranch a couple of days after offering that insight, toting his fly-fishing gear in one hand and a briefcase in the other, I had the feeling from the secretive, standoffish way he acted that he and my dad were hatching some plan to keep Acota out of our hair forever. When they disappeared into a mass of cottonwoods lining Willow Creek about a quarter mile from our house, fly rods and tackle boxes in hand, I felt a sense of both trepidation and envy. I knew they were looking for solace, just as I knew that their fishing expedition had more to do with business than pleasure. Nonetheless, the fact that I hadn't been asked to come along hurt, largely because I knew that if Jimmy had been alive, they would have asked him to join them. Deflated and recalling Spoon's earlier warning to be wary of Ricky, I decided to find some solace of my own and seek out Spoon's advice.

It took me a while, after stopping by the house to share my concerns about my dad and Ricky Peterson's secretiveness with my mom, to find Spoon on that cloudless evening. Summer had waned, and the chill of early fall was in the air. The cottonwoods along Willow Creek were a patchwork of muted greens and yellows as they marched toward their golden zenith.

I found Spoon in a pasture that had a small corral for breaking horses. He was standing in the middle of the corral, working Smokey on a twenty-foot lead. As I watched him work the big bay horse in a circle, widening the circle with each new pass, I realized he was trying to determine if Smokey had fully recovered from his injury.

"Move it, Smoke, move it," Spoon yelled, snapping the lead and stomping his foot.

When Smokey suddenly shifted gears and broke into a full-out, heads-up gallop, seeming to recognize for the first time that he was injury free, Spoon beamed. It took him several complete circles to break Smokey back down. By then I was sitting on the top rail of the corral, enjoying the show.

Still smiling and aware now that I was there, Spoon walked up to Smokey, snapped off the lead, and swatted him on the rump. Smokey took off in a blaze of speed, tearing around the corral like a colt.

"I'm thinkin' he's all well," Spoon said, walking toward me.

"I'm thinking you're right. My dad's gonna be real glad to stop having to ride Thunder."

Spoon nodded in agreement. "A man needs a mount that was built for him, and for your pa, that sure ain't Thunder. Where's he at anyway? Time for him and Smokey to get reacquainted."

"He's off fly-fishing with Ricky Peterson, or at least pretending to."

Spoon stared at me blankly.

"I don't like it," I said, feeding off the look on Spoon's

face. "They shut me out. My mom too. We're both real worried. I'm not so sure about Ricky's loyalty at this point. Think he could be tied to Acota?"

Spoon glanced briefly skyward, as if he might be searching for his answer there. "I've told you before, TJ, I ain't sure where he fits into all this. Haven't been able to get a real good read on the man. It ain't that he's the enemy so much as I tend to think he's inclined to offer up bad advice. And bad advice to a drownin' man lookin' to save his life by grabbin' on to a log that turns out to be an alligator is worse than no advice at all. Let me scratch around a bit and see if I can't get a handle on what Ricky and your pa are so busy strategizin' about."

"And what if they won't budge off their plans?"

"It's your pa's land to do with as he sees fit, TJ. And it's still him runnin' the coalition. Can't make him see or do things a different way if he don't want to."

"Guess so," I said, aware that if Spoon and I couldn't get my dad to let us in on what he and Ricky were up to, there was someone who could. I glanced back toward our house. In the fading light the house looked tiny, lost as it was against a towering expanse of cottonwoods. As I turned back and watched Spoon open a gate and send Smokey out to pasture, I wondered exactly what I would say to my mom.

△ △ △

Ricky and my dad came back from fishing a few minutes before dark. The summer's-end sound of chirping cicadas ended as they made their way across a meadow and toward the barn. Near the back of the barn they stopped and shook hands. From where I stood, hanging a halter in near darkness a few paces from the barn's open front door, I couldn't see their faces. But in the steely quiet, their words were absolutely clear.

"Sure hope your environmental angle works, Ricky," my dad said. "I'd hate to go to all this trouble and find out we still can't stop Acota. We're bettin' an awful lot on that twenty-plus-year recollection of yours."

"No argument there, Bill, but it's the soundest solution I can think of right now to keep Acota from gouging out the whole damn valley. That four hundred acres of BLM land you've been leasing all these years that's suddenly and mysteriously no longer available to you would let Acota get their foot right in the door. The law gives them the right to cross you once they have that lease. Next they'll grab up the adjacent two hundred acres of BLM ground that gives them access to the land they've leased from the Demasters, and you'll find yourself looking down the throat of a mining pit forever. It's your call, Bill."

When the cicadas suddenly started chirping again, it seemed louder than before. But not so loud that I couldn't make out my dad's response. "We'll go with your plan by week's end."

△ △ △

I'm not at all certain what my mom said to my dad that night, or if she even told him about my concerns. I don't know if they argued, discussed things calmly, or agreed to disagree, but the next morning at breakfast there was an obvious chill in the air. I wondered if she'd mentioned to him that I was the one with concerns about Ricky, or that, based on a conversation I'd had with Spoon of all people, Ricky might be the wrong person to be protecting our interests. I had no real way of knowing, as we sat in silence eating breakfast, where my dad might be placing blame, but from the way he kept casting looks of disappointment my mom's way, I was certain she was at the core of his upset.

We finished breakfast with fewer than half a dozen words spoken between us. As my dad and I headed out the kitchen door to meet Spoon, who'd saddled our horses in preparation for a seven-hour round-trip ride to gather 120 head of cattle from our south mesa meadow for sorting that evening and shipment the next day, my dad's parting words were, "Danged New Yorker!"

We left headquarters quickly, riding three abreast and barely speaking, toward the south mesa along with my dad's savvy five-year-old heeler, Duke, and my border collie, Cody. The two dogs streaked out ahead of us each time they caught a new, enticing scent until Spoon, sensing the tension in the air, asked, "Anything new with the Acota problem?" For some reason the dogs immediately stopped their antics.

My dad glanced over at me before answering. "We're working things out, me and Mr. Peterson."

"What about your coalition folks? Any stragglers?" Spoon asked, pressing the issue.

"We're dissolving the coalition. Too many points of view and vested interests to make it work."

Dad's response caught me by surprise. Spoon, however, seemed unfazed. He just shook his head and frowned. "So from here on out it's gonna be every man for himself?"

"Pretty close."

"Bad way to proceed."

"Don't you start with me, Spoon. I've had enough second-guessin' already. The decision was made on the advice of our attorney."

"Okay."

Eyeing Spoon sternly as if to say, *It better be*, dad glanced up at the sun. He could tell time by the sun as accurately as he could with a watch. "We've got cattle to gather, and time's a-wastin'. Let's get after it," he said, urging Smokey into a trot.

As Spoon and I took off after him, I knew there was little or no chance of rebuilding the Willow Creek Ranchers Coalition and that no matter what Ricky Peterson might be planning to take its place or to protect our ranch from Acota, there would be no changing my dad's mind on the issue.

△ △ △

Hours later, as we trailed a herd of reluctant-to-head-home mother cows and their calves back to headquarters with Cody and Duke nipping at the heels of the laggards, I reflected on the strange, out-of-character behavior my dad had shown as we'd gathered cattle. Like some tenderfoot bent on proving himself, he'd insisted on chasing down every breakaway calf and pinching every stubborn mother cow back into the herd by himself instead of letting the dogs do the work while we were up on the mesa. He'd barely taken a sip of water from his canteen the entire time, we'd never stopped for lunch, and he'd uttered fewer than a dozen words to Spoon and me in three hours. Only once, when Duke, insistent on doing his job in spite of my dad, lost his battle with a nervous calf who'd charged up a steep, sage-covered ditch bank, did Dad call for help. I ended up roping and dragging the kicking, bawling, five-hundred-pound steer back to the herd.

"Good show for a college kid," Dad had said with a wink. It was the only time all day that I had a normal sense of the man. Now, as I rode alongside him listening to our two cow dogs bark and yelp, I wondered how long it would be before Bill Darley returned.

△ △ △

By the time we finished dumping and sorting the cattle, a sharp evening chill was in the air. Mom, who'd stayed away from the sorting, unusual for her, surprised us all when she finally came out of the house. She headed directly across the wide swatch of grass that separated the house from the corrals. Dressed in jeans, boots, and a checkered wool shirt, she carried a handful of sweaters. Moving as always with the fluid grace of a dancer, she looked radiant. She was ten yards away from us when she called out, "I'm thinking the three of you must be hungry and a little on the chilly side by now."

"You can say that again, Mrs. D.," said Spoon.

"I whipped up something that I think will suit you."

She walked past Spoon and me toward my dad. "Hungry, Bill?" she asked, handing him one of the sweaters as he dismounted.

The way my dad said, "Absolutely," with a home-again air of graciousness, made me realize that whatever ugliness had passed between the two of them the previous evening was gone. Dad looped Smokey's reins around a fence post, and hugged mom tightly. I swore I heard him say sorry, but I couldn't be certain because whatever he'd said was cut short by the tender kiss my mom planted on his lips.

Turning unabashedly back toward me and Spoon and looking like a first-crush schoolgirl, Mom said, "Harriet Rankin came by this afternoon and left something for you, Spoon. Said it was terribly important that I give it to you as soon as you got back."

She reached into her shirt pocket, pulled out what was clearly a postcard, and handed it to Spoon. "Harriet said this came to her at the library, but it's definitely meant for you."

Spoon examined the postcard, which I later learned was simply addressed *Big Horn County Library, Hardin, Montana*, read the back of it, looked up at Mom wide eyed, and shook his head. "Looks like that old Cheyenne boy I spoke with up in Colstrip has had himself a change of heart. Seems like somethin's got him to admittin' we're kin."

I glanced at Spoon, then back at my folks. The joyful looks on their faces vanished when my mom said, "Harriet also left the information she said you wanted on Matt Rodue. It's back in the house. But I'm thinking right now we should all go and eat. Mr. Rodue's resume can wait, don't you think?"

"You're right on target there," said Spoon.

◁ ◁ ◁

An hour and two slices of pumpkin pie later, I was the last to read Harriet's summary of what she'd been able to find out about Matt Rodue. Spoon, then my dad, and finally my mom, who was now busy putting away dishes in the kitchen, had already read the two pages of neatly printed notes that Harriet had jotted on Big Horn County Library stationery. Her notes distilled the very essence of Matt Rodue.

Spoon and my dad were seated opposite one another in the matching wingback chairs that flanked the river-rock fireplace in our front room. Dad had recently taken to jokingly calling it our great room after seeing a similar room pictured on the cover of an exclusive log-homes magazine that featured multimillion-dollar second homes. I was seated on the sandstone hearth that spanned nearly three-quarters of the width of the room.

According to Harriet's notes, Matt Clarkson Rodue had been born thirty-seven years earlier in Joplin, Missouri, to a long-established farming family. He'd been a high school football star who'd attended the University of Missouri for a year before blowing out his right knee. Following that injury, Rodue had dropped out of football. He had later dropped out of school and spent the next several years back on the farm outside Joplin before going on to earn himself the reputation that had allowed Harriet to zero in on him so easily.

After leaving the farm, he hit the pro rodeo circuit and eventually became a highly regarded bull rider. A series of new knee injuries caused him to pack in that career, and he disappeared from the circuit, resurfacing several years later as one of the principals in a business that provided security for America's grandest pro rodeo events, including the Pendleton Round-Up, Cheyenne Frontier Days, and the Greeley Stampede.

It didn't appear that Harriet had had any difficulty unearthing facts about Rodue since, in her neat script near the bottom of the second page, she'd written,

> *See what you can find out with a little library research and the help of a friend who's been a lifelong rodeo fan? (Over)*

I flipped the page to see that Harriet had done some additional homework. In three lines she'd written down three more things she'd unearthed. As I read the three, the muscles in my neck tightened.

> *(1) Rodue wears gray because his great-grandfather was a general in Lee's army.*

(2) He's been reported to have a terrible, even sadistic
disposition that some fans think is related to the
fact that knee injuries cost him two careers.
(3) He's all about money.

I sat staring at the page until Spoon asked, "You all done with sizin' up Rodue, TJ?"

I choked out, "Yes."

"Bad hombre," Spoon said, enjoying the barest hint of an insightful smile.

"Sounds like it."

"You know what they say?" said Spoon. "The badder they are, the harder they fall."

I was all set to correct Spoon and remind him that it's "the bigger they are, the harder they fall," but his Cheshire-cat smile told me he was perfectly aware of his mistake.

"Think Rodue wants to take out any of his bitterness or his badness on us?" Dad asked.

"I ain't sure," said Spoon, massaging the cleft in his chin. "Guess we'll just have to wait and see."

The way Spoon said *wait*, as if the word carried with it some absolute assurance of things to come, caused my dad's eyes to widen, but not nearly as much or as expectantly as mine.

Sixteen

The Willow Creek Ranchers Coalition was dissolved by a show of hands during an early morning meeting that took place in our barn on the third Saturday of September 1991. It had snowed an inch at the ranch and six to eight inches in the surrounding mountains during the night, but an hour after sunrise the ranch's thirsty meadows were barely moist.

No one at the meeting seemed to want to call the question until my mom, dressed in jeans and an apron stained with tomato juice from the canning she and Harriet had been busy with back in the house, called out loud and clear, "I move we dissolve the coalition."

Ricky Peterson asked for a second to the motion, Maxine Cundiff provided a weak one, and just like that, on the heels of an all-in-favor call from Ricky, the coalition died. I couldn't say I was unhappy. Disappointed seemed to be a better description. I'd learned from experience what it meant to go up against a force stronger than you and lose. My basketball team's loss in the state championship final my senior year to a Bozeman team with a high school all-American had shown me the way. But not before I'd learned to fully appreciate the concept of teamwork and what it meant to make it to a place no one ever expected you to get to on the basis of sheer desire rather than skill.

There was something about the way the ranchers in our valley had thrown up their hands in the face of Acota Energy's looming presence that bothered me. Something sickening that as much as shouted, *Forget about the other guy as long as I get mine.*

As far as I was concerned, only my dad's reasons for bowing out seemed reasonable. He was tired of being the lightning rod between the coalition and Acota. Tired of driving—sometimes three times a week—to meet with Ricky Peterson in Billings. Tired of trying to defend Willard Johnson's death as an accident while everyone else continued to whisper that Johnson had more than likely been killed by Matt Rodue. Most of all he seemed tired of the sniping and backbiting. The Cundiffs had suggested that he and Ricky Peterson were working on a separate deal with Acota that would give the energy giant a right to encroach on us in order to mine surrounding government lands, and that as part of the deal we would earn encroachment royalties that could potentially pay us thirty percent more than anyone else in the valley could get for the right to strip-mine. My dad and Ricky had assured everyone that the encroachment issue was no more than a rumor, probably started by the Acota people themselves, but they'd had one hell of a time trying to get people to believe them.

With nothing more than a lingering bad taste and bad feelings all around, the meeting ended with everyone shuffling out of the barn, grumbling like a bunch of kids who'd all been in favor of going to see a movie until they had to decide what movie to see.

Ralph Cundiff was a half step ahead of me and my dad as we moved toward the barn doors. "Guess it's every man for himself at this point," he mumbled. "Sure hope nobody ends up with a competitive edge here. Wouldn't be right, maybe not even legal." His comment was aimed at Ricky Peterson, but he was looking directly at my dad.

"No one's going to have any negotiating advantage with Acota, Ralph," Ricky said, sounding exasperated.

"And it wouldn't matter anyway, since they won't be diggin' on this ranch, ever," said my dad. "As far as I'm concerned, they can start their earth gougin' with you, Ralph. So negotiate your best deal and let 'em eviscerate your damn place."

"No need for all the testiness, Bill," Cundiff said, holding up a protective hand.

Looking disgusted, my dad shook his head and walked away.

I followed him and Ricky from the barn to where Spoon, my mom, and Harriet Rankin stood talking. Dad barely slowed his pace as he brushed past everyone with Ricky still in tow. "I've washed my hands of it," he grumbled. "From now on, every rancher in this valley's on their own." He and Ricky disappeared into the house.

Within five more minutes everyone had said their good-byes and departed, leaving my mom, Spoon, Harriet, and me outside talking. The temperature was in the low forties, and our frosted breaths megaphoned out from our mouths as we talked.

"So what do you think will happen now?" Harriet asked my mom, looking around at the landscape. "Do you think Acota will really come out here and soil this beautiful place?"

Mom shrugged and looked at Spoon. "You're the prognosticator, Spoon. What's your take?"

Spoon continued to chew on the toothpick that jutted from the right corner of his mouth. Against a backdrop of sunlight, he looked taller, leaner, and even more insightful than normal. His long, wiry hair drifted back and forth in the breeze, and his unblemished, cocoa brown skin seemed to glisten. "I'm thinkin' Acota will whittle away at you one by one, bit by bit. Try and peck away at every rancher in this valley hopin' to get what they want, sorta like a vulture peckin' at a carcass."

Looking sad-eyed but defiant, my mom said, "Until the valley ends up stinking to high heaven and spewing sulfur fumes, no more than a bottomless pit of coal. I sure hope not."

"I didn't say they'd succeed, Mrs. D. Just said they'd try. There's lots of ways to keep the wolf from your door. Let me think on it a bit. Maybe I can come up with somethin' to take Acota off your scent."

Harriet flashed Spoon a reel-in-your-sails kind of look that told me that she very likely had a deeper understanding of Mr. Arcus Witherspoon than I expected. "Just make sure that whatever you're thinking about doing is legal, Arcus."

"Wouldn't dream of havin' it any other way." Spoon flashed her a mischievous smile.

"I suppose you plan to deal with Acota when you're not working or off somewhere searching out your roots," Harriet said.

"Sure am. That old boy up in Colstrip who sent me that postcard all drippin' with guilt is supposed to meet me in Butte in a couple of days. Claims he'll lay out all he knows about our family tree on the spot. I'll finish tracin' out the rest on my own. When I talked to him on the phone yesterday, he sounded pretty sincere."

"Sure seems strange," said Harriet. "His sudden change of heart, I mean. One day he's disowning you, and the next day he's your closest kin. What happened?"

"I ain't really sure. Maybe he felt bad about lyin' to me the first time we met. Or maybe he wants to get at the bottom of his own family history as bad as I do. All I know is we're gonna talk."

"I sure hope that talk gets you to where you want to be," said my mom.

"I'm thinkin' it will," said Spoon. "In the meantime, I'll be studyin' your dilemma, Mrs. D. Mullin' over how to keep them vultures from Acota from collapsin' down on you and yours. I'll come up with somethin' for sure," he said, turning to face Harriet. "You about ready to head back into town, Harriet?"

"You need me to help you with anything else here, Marva?" Harriet asked.

"Nope. We're done for the season as far as I'm concerned."

"Then I guess I'll head back to Hardin," Harriet said, sounding as if she didn't really want to leave. "Just let me get my things from the house."

She and my mom headed indoors. They'd reached the front porch when I said to Spoon, "Real nice lady, Harriet."

"Extra nice." Spoon smiled, pivoted, and stared skyward. "And knowledgeable," he added. "Told me as soon as she got out here to the ranch today that she'd done a little more studyin' up on Matt Rodue. Turns out I'm not the only ex-con with a fondness for your valley. According to Harriet, Rodue did nine months of hard time back in Missouri for aggravated assault. Wonder what Sheriff Woodson has up his sleeve for dealin' with two ex-cons."

"You've got me."

Spoon shrugged. There was a hint of bitterness in what he said next. "I just hope he tattooed Rodue with as many questions about Willard Johnson's death as he did me."

As I saw it, Spoon's bitterness was well deserved. Woodson had ambushed him, as much as locked him down in his quarters one evening a couple of days after Willard's death, and peppered him for a good two hours with questions concerning his whereabouts on the night before and morning of Willard's death. Spoon's next words stayed with me for the rest of the day.

"But then again, Rodue ain't nearly as black nor half as Indian as me."

It was the only time since I'd met him that I'd ever known Spoon to allow the question of race and its direct effect on him to filter its way into a conversation. I could tell from the pained expression on his face that no matter how much he might try to explain the reasons for what I realized was genuine anger, he couldn't make me understand.

As quickly as his anger peaked, it was gone. "No matter," he said with a dismissive shrug, locking eyes with me. "The important thing to remember in life is that regardless of how bad you might end up gettin' treated, don't never let nobody with an agenda stop your train from makin' it to where it's goin'." He glanced toward his pickup, where Harriet now sat patiently waiting. "Gotta roll, TJ. See ya later." Adjusting his Stetson, he headed to the truck and got in.

As the truck rolled off, I knew that I'd just seen a side of Spoon that he kept well hidden. A side that was capable of taking him back to places he didn't want to go. I also had the feeling that he'd never let me see that side of him again.

△ △ △

While Spoon had promised to think about how to best deal with Acota, it turned out that Ricky Peterson and my dad had been working on strategies of their own. I was barely in the back door of the house when my mom waved to me from the kitchen and said, just above a whisper, "TJ, step in here for a minute. I need to talk to you about something."

I stepped from the mudroom into the kitchen, still mulling over why Sheriff Woodson likely hadn't taken it upon himself to grill Matt Rodue the same way he'd grilled Spoon and choking on my own anger since I knew exactly why. Then I noticed the ponderous look on my mom's face. That look, one Dad liked to refer to as "New York serious," was one I'd never been able to get used to. It was a look that Dad always claimed had totally enchanted him when as a young navy seaman he'd first seen my mom onstage in a chorus line of June Taylor dancers.

Looking around as if she thought someone might be watching or listening, Mom said, "Did Spoon and Harriet get off okay?"

The way she phrased the question, as if it were some kind of courtroom preamble to where she really intended the conversation to go, caused me to stop short.

"They're a good match, Spoon and Harriet. Don't you think?"

"Yeah, but I don't think Spoon appreciates the scrutiny."

Mom smiled. "You know what, TJ? I don't much care what Spoon thinks. At least not on that issue. More often than not, it's the most jagged rock in the river that requires the strongest stream force to smooth it out. If Spoon doesn't want me asking about him and Harriet, then he shouldn't offer to transport her out here to the ranch. But that's not what I want to discuss with you," she said, corralling her emotions and glancing toward my dad's study, where he and Ricky remained sequestered. "I need to talk to you about something that has me terribly worried. Something I think Ricky and your dad might be planning. They've been far too secretive for their own good lately, and it's bothering me to the point that it has me thinking about your brother, Jimmy, and things that happened a long time ago. You know, it's been years since I've really thought about Ricky and Jimmy and that fire down at the gas seep that left Ricky's arm pretty much useless."

She tried to force back a frown, but one came anyway. I could tell by the look of anguish on her face that she'd been struggling to keep from going back to what she called one of life's dark places. "Ricky was one heck of a trouper after that fire," she said finally. "Wrapped up in gauze from his belly button to his neck like he was—hurting to high heaven and never once complaining. That boy's skin flaked and oozed for close to a year, and he never once turned angry—never once sloshed around in self-pity. Then again, he comes from the kind of stock that wouldn't have permitted it. He and your dad are a lot alike, you know."

"Yeah, I know." I wanted to add, "And Ricky's a lot like Jimmy," but I didn't.

Looking more nervous by the second, she said, "For some reason I've got this horrible feeling that the two of them are conjuring up something that can't turn out well for any of us. That fire at the seep all those years back forged a pact between them that you might say is unhealthy. Ricky's guilt over starting a fire that left him permanently injured and almost got Jimmy killed is the kind of guilt that won't let him say no to the father of his long-dead best friend, and your dad's no better. I think he sees Jimmy's reflection in Ricky." She let out a sigh. "They're planning something dangerous, TJ, I know it. Something so dangerous that I think it could end up costing us this land. I need you to help me find out what it is and help me stop them."

"What's got you convinced they're planning something so serious?"

Her eyes to the floor, she walked over to the kitchen drawer where she kept bottle openers, corkscrews, and bag clips. Her eyes darted from side to side as she pulled the drawer open. "I found something your dad left lying on a workbench in the barn the other evening. It was there when I went out to get some of my canning supplies."

She shoved the drawer's contents to one side, lifted the drawer liner, slipped several sheets of paper from beneath the liner, and handed them to me. "I want you to read what's on those pages carefully, TJ, top to bottom, and tell me what you think. It's had me worried something terrible for almost two days."

When I pulled up a stool to sit down and read the paper-clipped pages, she said, "No! Read it in your bedroom. We'll talk about what you've read in the morning." Her voice wavered as she spoke, and suddenly her nervousness became mine.

"Okay," I said, draping a reassuring arm over her shoulders.

"Run along, now, before your dad comes in here and gets to wondering what we're talking about and why I came to you with what's in that article instead of him."

I glanced down at the headline on the top of the first piece of paper: "Fire in the Hole." The title didn't mean much to me, but a little later, as I slowly read through the article in my room, I found myself shivering in fear and sharing my mom's concern.

Seventeen

After spending the rest of the day second-guessing my dad, sharing the guilt my mom must have felt over invading his privacy, and running the contents of the "Fire in the Hole" article through my head like a newsreel, over and over until I knew its contents by heart, I had a good idea of what Ricky and my dad were up to.

When I reread, in the privacy of my room that night, the seven pages of the *Science and Nature* magazine article that had run the previous November, it no longer seemed dry and boring, as it had during the day, or for that matter just another scholarly paper spelling out the hellishness that could result from underground coal fires. It seemed real.

My dad had highlighted a paragraph in yellow that pointed out that China and India, with the largest number of coal fires in the world, had done little to combat them. Only the United States had made attempts to manage such fires, which were most rampant in America's oldest eastern coalfields. Few fires, it seemed, had ever extinguished themselves.

It was a paragraph near the end of the article that gave me a better sense of what my dad and Ricky might be planning. That paragraph explained that underground fires produced subsidence, or cave-in, zones that made coal mining dangerous, if not impossible, within fifty miles of the zones. In legalistic language, the article went on to state that no coal mining of any sort was allowed on government-owned lands, including BLM land, national forest property, or adjacent private property judged to be at risk for subsidence and the spread of underground coal fires. A footnote listed two federal statutes forbidding anyone to mine such sites, noting that such actions were a criminal violation and that violators would be subject to a $100,000 fine per site and five years in jail.

I was fearful that my dad and Ricky were planning to keep Acota out of our valley and off our land by starting an underground coal fire. I couldn't imagine how two normally right-thinking men could have come up with such a risky scheme, but the more I thought about it, the more I found myself believing it was possible that they had. I spent the next hour or so trying to come up with a logical rationale for such a scheme before drifting off to sleep at four in the morning.

I woke up in a sweat, uncertain just how long I'd been dreaming about my dad's navy experience as a Seabee and demolitions expert. I'd seen him take out hillsides with half a dozen well-placed charges of dynamite in order to control soil erosion without disturbing a single wild-flower on the adjacent hill. I'd watched him cut in miles of right-of-way for fence with a road grader or a back-hoe and barely brush a rabbit hole. I'd seen him burn off fifty-acre patches of cow-clinging thistle and toxic spurge before stopping the fire line on a dime with a perfect backburn and several loader buckets full of well-placed dirt. If anyone could start a fire and then turn around and either blast or bulldoze the life out of it, which was what I suspected he and Ricky ultimately had in mind, there was no question Dad could.

Even so, the risk seemed disproportionate to any possible gain. He'd be starting a fire he might not be able to stop. A fire that could leave behind smoldering pits, tree stumps venting smoke, and fissures spewing flames from the ground forever.

When the scheme I'd been conjuring up for most of a day began to make no sense to me, I quietly left my room just before six and headed for Spoon's quarters to get his take on the nightmare I imagined.

I found Spoon wide awake in his room packing, of all things, a lunch. He didn't seem all that surprised to see me.

"Ham and swiss on rye," he said with a smile, topping off a ham sandwich with a double layer of cheese and a slice of Jewish rye. "Fit for a king. First thing I had when I landed in San Francisco on my way back from 'Nam."

As he wrapped the sandwich in wax paper, I spotted two more neatly wrapped sandwiches lying next to a cooler on the old carpenter's chest he used for a coffee table. Remembering that it was Spoon's day off, I asked, "Where are you headed?"

"Searchin' out my roots, what else?" he said before setting his sandwich aside, eyeing me pensively, and asking, "Pretty early in the mornin' to be runnin' me down. You got a problem, TJ?"

Uncertain how to broach the subject, I said, "Yes. It's about my dad."

"He got you bentonitin' ditches again?" Spoon asked with a chuckle, aware that I hated riding the endless miles of our irrigation ditches and sealing up cracks and potential leaks with the sticky, claylike dike plugger called bentonite.

"Nope."

"Then what?" Spoon asked, taking in the weighty look on my face.

My answer came in a rush. "I think my dad and Ricky Peterson have cooked up some crazy scheme to try and keep Acota out of here by starting an underground coal fire."

Spoon eyed me with disbelief. "Don't make no sense to me," he said, placing his sandwiches in the cooler. "Nope, no way they'd do that at all."

"I've been telling myself the same thing for almost a day now." I slipped the neatly folded "Fire in the Hole" article out of my back pocket and handed it to him. "Have a look at this."

Spoon glanced at his watch. "Afraid I'm gonna have to make it quick. I'm meetin' Harriet in town at the Merry Mixer for breakfast, and then we're headed up to talk to that toothless old geezer in Colstrip about him bein' my kin."

Spoon pulled a stool up next to the carpenter's chest and quickly read through the article. Seconds after finishing, he let out a sigh. "Sounds to me like we don't want any part of no coal fire. You might as well spray this valley with Agent Orange."

He handed the article back to me. "What makes you so blessed sure that Ricky and your pa are planning to start one?"

"Just a hunch, and my mom agrees. I think Dad's planning to use his demolition experience to start a fire and then put it out. Once there's a documented subsidence fire, Acota will never be able to mine this land."

"And I think you're way off base," Spoon said, shaking his head, walking across the room, and extracting a couple of sodas from the dented refrigerator he'd bought at a farm auction the previous summer. "I'd say it's more likely that he and Ricky are lookin' for some legal way to keep Acota outta here."

"Could be," I said with a shrug, feeling relieved. "But how do you think I can find out?"

Spoon smiled and placed the soda in his cooler. "I'd ask your pa."

"But he'll know that Mom and I took the article and read it. She found it lying out on a workbench."

"Then he shouldn'ta left it lying around." Clearly preoccupied, he eyed his watch again. "Sorry, TJ, I gotta go." He picked up the cooler and headed for the door. Looking back at me, he said, "Talk to your pa."

As the screen door creaked open, I asked, "Think that old Cheyenne guy up in Colstrip will tell you the whole truth this time around?"

"I'm hopin' he will. Hate to waste a trip. As for the truth—like they say, it can set you free. Go talk to your pa about that article. The truth'll come out."

Spoon was down the tack room's two rickety porch steps and halfway to his pickup when I decided I might as well go talk to my dad right then.

As Spoon nosed his pickup down the lane and toward

the county road, I saw my dad, with his right foot planted on an old cottonwood stump, several yards back from the lane. Up and out at first light, as was his custom, he held a coffee mug in his hand. Thinking, *It's now or never*, I waved at him and trotted his way. His return wave seemed halfhearted. Shifting his left foot up onto the stump just as I reached him, he said, "See Spoon's outta here real early."

"He's going to pick up Harriet. They're headed up to Colstrip to meet with some old Cheyenne guy. Spoon claims he and the old man are kin."

"Thinkin' somethin's true doesn't make it so."

"Guess so," I said, determined to charge right into the coal-fire issue. Reaching into my back pocket, I pulled out the article. "I found this lyin' around," I said, nearly stuttering. "It's a piece on underground coal fires."

"Oh. And what did you learn from it?" Dad barely sounded surprised.

"That they can be devastating and that they can burn just about forever."

"That all?"

"Nope. There's a section that talks about natural gas fires and coal fires competing. Seems like sometimes they're able to snuff one another out. Sorta end up in a draw."

"Like lots of things in life. Where'd you find that article?" he asked.

"Ah…in the dining room."

"Strange. I don't remember leaving it there."

"Well…"

He stepped forward and draped an arm over my shoulder. "You can stop hemmin' and hawin' and coverin' for your mom, TJ. She came clean earlier this morning. Told me she was the one who found the article and read it." He sighed and shook his head. "What surprises the heck outta me is how fast the two of you eased down a crooked back road to nowhere after readin' that piece. Let me set you straight. First off, like I told your mom, I'm not plannin' on startin' any fires, puttin' any out, or, God forbid, blowin' anything up. What Ricky and I are hopin' to do is get an injunction that will stop Acota from strip-mining any of the ranches that meet at Four Corners by arguin' that mining these lands will put every rancher involved at risk for underground fires and damage to the ecosystem." He looked at me and smiled. "No need to conjure up ghosts when there aren't any, TJ. Now, does that set things straight for you?"

I don't remember letting out a sigh of relief, but I'm sure I must have.

When he continued, his tone was a little more biting. "This time you, your mom, and Spoon were way off base. I can understand Spoon's continued need to prognosticate, given that supposedly clairvoyant bone of his, but you and your mom should know better."

It was easy to see why he figured that Spoon had been a party to the hysteria, since he'd just seen me coming from Spoon's quarters. Determined not to allow Spoon to be tarred with the same brush as Mom and me, I said, "Spoon didn't have anything to do with me and Mom jumping to conclusions. We did that on our own."

"Maybe not directly," Dad said, shaking his head. "But he's the one who's got the two of you in some constant prophesyin' frame of mind. We've hoed this row before, TJ, and I've told you that Spoon's so-called future-seein' powers are nothin' but a fulcrum for trouble. So if you and your mom would do me the favor of a little less conjurin', I'd sure appreciate it."

"Okay."

He nodded approvingly, the way he generally did when a bargain had been struck. "Good," he said, glancing toward the county road. "Sure hope Spoon finds what he's lookin' for. But you know what? I don't think he's ever gonna. Men like Spoon aren't meant to find balance, or for that matter very much satisfaction, in this world. If they did, it would probably ruin 'em."

He removed the railroad engineer's cap he always wore for welding and snapped the dust off the brim. "How about helping me weld a few loose pipe joints in the corrals?"

"Sure thing. I'll go get goggles and gloves." I headed for the machine shop to get the gear. Halfway to the shop I glanced toward the house and realized that my mom had been watching our conversation from the front porch. I flashed her a thumbs-up sign, and she responded with a smile. When I reached the shop, I wondered if she and Dad had had the same conversation about jumping to conclusions, underground coal fires, and the divisiveness caused by Spoon's predictions, and I wondered if in the future she'd be less likely to conjure up boogeymen when there weren't any there.

Eighteen

I'd never met Willard Johnson's niece—in fact, until his death I'd never even heard of her. But just after lunch on the day Spoon took off for Colstrip, Thelma Lawson, the daughter and only child of Willard Johnson's long-deceased brother, showed up at our ranch with her husband, a small-ish, rumpled, bug-eyed wisp of a man, in tow.

I was sitting on our front porch with my folks when they arrived in a gunmetal gray Suburban sporting tempo-rary plates. We were lined up three abreast, enjoying the eighty-year-old wooden porch swing that had belonged to my grandfather and discussing neither the defunct Willow Creek Ranchers Coalition nor greedy, coal-excavating companies looking to strip-mine us out of existence, but instead what Spoon and Harriet might be up to romanti-cally. My mom had started us down that road by mention-ing that Harriet, as giddy as a schoolgirl, had called that morning to tell her that she was more than a little nervous about making the Colstrip trip with Spoon.

Dad's tongue-in-cheek response to her revelation, "Songbird's gotta sing, Marva. Could be Harriet's got a lot more chirp in her than she generally lets on," came just as the Suburban pulled to a stop in front of the house.

Trying her best to keep a straight face, Mom said, "Bill, please," as she rose to greet the SUV's occupants.

Thelma Lawson was a big-boned, russet-skinned woman. Her hair was in a tight bun, and she wore unbecoming tortoiseshell glasses. She walked straight up the porch steps as if she'd been there before, introduced herself as Willard Johnson's niece, and, turning daintily toward the man below her on the steps, announced, "This is my husband, Jarvon."

Jarvon stood there without moving, right hip cocked higher than the left, and forced a smile.

"Well, hello," my mom said, still not completely comfortable after all her time out west with a simple howdy.

I had the feeling as I stared down at Jarvon that no matter the time, the place, or the circumstance, he always remained at least three steps below or behind his wife.

"I'm hoping you're the Darleys," Thelma said. Her voice had the telltale hoarseness of a long-term smoker. She smiled at each of us before flashing Jarvon a look that said, *I told you so.*

"That we are," Mom said, shaking hands with Thelma, then stretching to shake hands with Jarvon. As my dad and I moved to greet the Lawsons, Thelma never moved from her perch on the top porch step, and Jarvon never ascended from his.

"Why don't you join us on the porch and visit for a bit?" Mom asked as the handshaking ended.

"We'd like to," Thelma said, looking down at Jarvon as if to say, *I'll do the talking.* "But we've got several more stops to make in the valley. We just stopped by to let you know that we've leased my uncle's coal rights to Acota Energy. Thought you had a right to know."

None of us were surprised by the revelation. I was, however, curious why Thelma kept referring to herself as "we" when Jarvon more than likely had zero input into any decision his wife made.

Continuing as if she were in a classroom lecturing, Thelma said, "I didn't want people down here in this valley to get all riled up over my leasing the ranch out to Acota and end up trashing my uncle's place. So I figured I'd come by and tell everybody personally what we'd done."

My mom's tone, which to that point had been hospitable, took a sharp, unfriendly U-turn. "I don't think anyone in this valley would care to trash Willard's property, Mrs. Lawson. Besides, it would be pretty hard to trash all that acreage, unless of course you leased it out to a strip-mining company."

I nearly said, "Oh, shit," as my dad stepped forward to intervene. Thelma Lawson might have been accustomed to raining down orders on the little man standing below her on the steps, but the cold hostility in my mom's voice signaled that Thelma was teetering on the brink of an old-fashioned verbal butt-whipping.

My dad smiled at my mom, who was now an irritated shade of pink, and slipped his arm around her waist. "We appreciate your stoppin' by and givin' us a heads-up," he said to Thelma. He sounded so ingratiating that I could've sworn he was the one who'd been a Broadway entertainer, not Mom. "Who else do you plan on visitin'?" he asked, squeezing my obviously ruffled mom more tightly.

"The Cundiffs, Dale Turpin for sure, and Thurston

Lyle, if time permits," Thelma said in what could only be described as a snit.

Still seething, my mom flashed both Lawsons her best chorus-line-dancer's smile. "Well, please give them our best."

Dad and I broke into disingenuous smiles of our own.

Uncertain what to make of the three mind-melded faces smiling at her, Thelma glared down at Jarvon. "I think we're done here," she said authoritatively.

As Jarvon's head bobbed up and down, like an excited puppy's, and he turned to leave, my dad slipped his right hand into my mom's and squeezed it tightly. He might as well have just come out and said, "Don't you dare say anything, Marva; just let them leave." My mom's smile turned into an ice-dagger stare as Thelma turned and bounded down the porch steps. Jarvon schlepped his way to the Suburban two steps behind her. Only when the engine roared to life did I realize that my dad was restraining my mom by the waist.

"The nerve!" Mom said as the Suburban circled the driveway.

Eyeing me and trying his best not to laugh, Dad simply said, "Yep."

"Don't you dare laugh, Bill Darley!" Thoroughly peeved, Mom slipped out of his grasp, my dad swallowed his laugh, and I was left to enjoy an inward chuckle, knowing Thelma Lawson wasn't the only person who could turn her husband on a dime.

△ △ △

We didn't say much about the Lawsons' visit until two days later, when it became obvious to every rancher in the valley that, given the speed of Acota's negations with Thelma, Acota and Willard Johnson had been working on a leasing agreement for quite a while before his death. That same day, Spoon, who'd been strangely standoffish since returning from his meeting in Colstrip, walked into our machine shop, a little past nine, where Dad and I were busy replacing a set of blades on one of our hay mowers, and announced that a dozer, several front-end loaders, a couple of road graders, a strip-mining bucket and dragline, and three backhoes were lined up like *Star Wars* mechanical beasts on Willard Johnson's property just up from Four Corners, about thirty yards from our fence line.

"Acota's settin' up to dig," Spoon said, nodding to himself as if there were some need to confirm the statement. "And from the looks of things, I'd say pretty quick. Might take 'em a while to set up that dragline and bucket, but from what I saw, they could be in business within a week."

My dad set his socket wrench aside on a bench top. The look on his face was more one of calculation than upset or anger.

"I rode our Four Corners quarter section three days back. Wasn't no equipment there then," Spoon said, pointedly.

"They must've moved it in since then," my dad said. "Probably at night for fear we'd see them."

"No matter. Their equipment's still on Willard's side of the fence," I said.

"Yeah. But the question is how'd it get there? It's a hell of a lot longer and a much more risky trip to bring equipment like that around the backside of Willard's. Cross us and you save yourself at least a day and the chance of gettin' mired in the creek."

"And that's just what they did," Spoon chimed in. "Cut across us. There's plenty of tracks out there to prove it. Means they musta done a lot of their movin' durin' that rain we had a few days back. There's one other thing," he added reluctantly. "There's a thirty-foot-long diesel-fuel spill just up from the gas seep. You can smell it from a good bit away. They musta tipped a fuel tank or piece of equipment over in their rush."

"Bold move, though, you gotta give 'em that," Dad said, deep in thought.

"Yeah." Spoon adjusted his Stetson. "Bold enough to make me think Acota's lookin' to provoke us."

"Or lookin' to flex enough muscle that we'll turn tail and run."

"How could they have gotten a go-ahead to dig so fast?" I asked.

Dad shook his head. "Who knows? Maybe Acota greased the right palms, or maybe they worked out a deal that got approval while Willard was still alive. Could be that all that irritatin' niece of his had to do after his death to get the deal on a fast track was to dot a few i's and cross a few t's. Especially if he'd already named her as executor of his estate should anything ever happen to him."

"Sounds like you've done some thinkin' on the subject," Spoon said.

"I have, but mainly I'm just repeatin' some of the things Ricky Peterson laid out as possibilities a couple of weeks back."

"So what do we do?" I asked.

"For the moment, nothin'," Dad said. "At least not until I've had a chance to talk to Ricky. I'm guessin' right now that the most we can hope for legally would be for a judge to fine Acota for trespassin'. And when you get right down to it, what would they care? The fine would be two or three thousand dollars at the most. It would cost me as much in attorney's fees to make an issue of it."

He leaned back against the workbench and rubbed his hands together, almost in anticipation, it seemed to me. "There's somethin' else at stake here, though. Somethin' bigger than petty fines for trespassin', or the fact that Acota's primed to forever scar up this valley. And that's the fact that we're dealin' with bullies. Flat-out, second-grade, kick-sand-in-your-face kind of bullies. Arrogant asses who think they can do anything they please."

Spoon's and Dad's nearly synchronous nods and their identical determined looks told me that for once they were on the very same line of the very same page.

"I'm thinkin' it's time the folks at Acota get taught a lesson," Dad said. "One that just might keep them from pullin' the same shenanigans elsewhere. Whatta you think, Spoon?"

I had the sense all of a sudden that both men had forgotten I was there. They seemed to be communicating in some between-the-lines kind of language I couldn't understand. As they eyed one another with an earnestness I'd rarely seen, I had the feeling they were thinking, *Let's lob a grenade or two and even the score.* I fought back a shiver as I considered running from the shop and shouting to someone in authority, as if I were some schoolchild on a playground, "Do you know what Arcus Witherspoon and Bill Darley are planning to do?" Instead, I stood and watched my dad and Spoon continue to connect in a way that I imagined soldiers thrown together by happenstance and bonded by necessity likely did.

△ △ △

Dad didn't say anything to Mom about what had transpired in the machine shop as the three of us ate lunch a few hours later. He'd talked to Ricky Peterson by phone, I knew that much. But he wasn't tipping his hand for dealing with Acota. As we wolfed down a meal of biscuits and honey, meatloaf sandwiches, and vegetable soup, I had the sense that Dad was weighing all his options.

"Get either of you seconds?" my mom asked, noting my dad's thoughtful mood.

"Nope," Dad said.

"Something the matter, Bill?" she asked. "Your jaws seem a little tight." It was a catchphrase she used whenever my dad seemed stubbornly preoccupied.

"Nope."

"Doesn't look that way to me. In fact, you and TJ both seem a little tight jawed to me."

For a second I thought Dad might mention Spoon's early morning trespassing revelation, but before he could, Mom said, "Now, Spoon being preoccupied, I can understand. Especially now that he's discovered that searching out his roots might very likely take him off to Washington State, or maybe even Alaska."

"How's that?" I asked, totally surprised.

"You mean Spoon didn't tell either of you about what happened on that trip up to Colstrip?"

"No," I said, feeling the muscles in my gut tighten.

"I'm surprised by that. Real surprised. Anyway, what he found out is that he's related to that old Cheyenne man, all right, but not in a way he figured. It turns out, at least according to what Harriet has told me, that the woman Spoon's great-grandfather was supposedly married to wasn't Cheyenne at all. According to what the old man told Spoon, she was Muckleshoot, or possibly even Yakama, and she'd been taken in by the old man's family after losing both her parents as a child."

"What about that land Spoon talked about?" I asked. "The land Spoon's kin supposedly owned up at Powder River Bluff?"

"Harriet claims the land's his, all right, but he'll have to do a lot of legal legwork to claim it."

"Ricky Peterson can help," I blurted out.

"I'm sure he can," Mom said. "But I expect it's really not the land that Spoon's after. He's looking for the genesis of his family, not simply a piece of real estate. Harriet says he's terribly disappointed, especially since he thought he was close to the end of his search."

"So what's he plan to do?" my dad asked.

"He hasn't told anyone. Right now he's got Harriet doing a title search on that piece of land."

"Think he might leave?" I asked.

"I don't really know," Mom said.

"I'd hate to lose him. At this point especially," Dad said.

Uncomfortable with the possibility that Spoon might leave, I said, "Can't you get Ricky to help, please?"

Sensing that I was upset, Dad leaned over from his seat and patted me reassuringly on the shoulder. "We'll work this out, TJ," he said. But the way he said it didn't give me any confidence that we would.

△ △ △

I spent the rest of the day working on machinery, greasing tractor rear ends, checking tires, batteries, fan belts, and alternators, and mothballing equipment that wouldn't be needed until spring. I didn't think much about my dad or Spoon's leaving during the four hours or so it took me to finish the tasks, largely because, engaging a self-protective trait I'd perfected over the years, I forced myself not to. When I headed from the machine shop to the barn to get the coffee can full of assorted nuts and bolts that I'd left there earlier, I found myself thinking about college and the fact that I'd be leaving Willow Creek come January.

Nineteen

I finished up in the machine shop and was busy crisscrossing one of our bull pastures on an ATV, tagging lingering toxic weeds with orange marker dye so Spoon could come back and spray them later, when I caught sight of what looked like smoke rising in the distance. Fire, flood, and livestock disease are the three things no rancher ever wants to encounter, so I made a beeline for the smoke, losing my hat, my marker dye, and a set of socket wrenches in a chase that had me headed straight to Four Corners.

Ten minutes later, with my ribs throbbing from the jarring they'd taken as a result of my full-throttle crossing of the rough, rocky terrain, I found myself listening to the rumble of diesel engines and staring at exhaust smoke. My first thought as I pulled to a stop and watched the smoke rise was that Spoon had brought a backhoe down to Four Corners to dig up some boulders and move them to a nearby dry wash that had a tendency to erode from the mountain snow runoff each spring. When I rose from my seat and glanced over a rise to look down on Four Corners, I saw what Spoon had been so concerned about that morning. Half a dozen pieces of heavy equipment stared back up at me. The earth-moving armada was assembled in a semicircle on Willard Johnson's property, about thirty yards north of our fence line, spewing the smoke I'd seen. The Acota Energy logo was stenciled on the door or hood of every piece of machinery.

I didn't see the one-ton pickup that my dad and Spoon had retrofitted the previous winter with a flat bed and a new Dodge hemi engine until I started down the hill toward the Four Corners survey pin. The pickup was parked a few feet from our fence. My dad was standing in front of the truck with one arm extended due west toward a stand of nearby aspen. Spoon stood motionless on the flatbed looking toward where my dad was pointing. As I accelerated toward them, I wondered how long they had been there.

I was twenty yards downwind from the flatbed when I remembered that my dad and Spoon had retrofitted the truck with two other things: a carpet-lined aluminum tool tote and a headache rack. During the fall and hunting season, the tote was used to store rifles and shotguns.

My dad lowered his arm and looked my way when I pulled the ATV to a stop a few feet from the flatbed. Motioning for me to stay seated, he called across the fence to a large, bearded man in coveralls and a small, balding man standing at his side, "I'm gonna ask you one last time how you brought that equipment of yours in here before I ask Mr. Witherspoon up there on the flatbed to remedy the situation."

The bearded man, who I could now see was chomping on a cigar, said, "We moved it from the backside of this here property it's sittin' on, and like I told you, we're just testing it out."

Dad shook his head in protest. "Then where in hell did all the heavy-equipment tire tracks and the diesel-fuel spill that runs pretty much all the way down to our seep over there come from?" His tone, one I'd heard plenty of times when I'd been the subject of his interrogation, was searing.

"Can't say as I know," the man in coveralls said, sucking on his cigar and blowing out a puff of smoke before turning to grin broadly at his associate, who erupted in laughter. As they both laughed, I realized there were two men seated in the cab of a smoke-spewing road grader that was about fifteen paces away, taking in the show.

My dad's determined gaze moved from the two men on the ground slowly up to the men in the grader, then back to Spoon. Nodding at Spoon, he said, "I'm thinking these gents from Acota need to learn to start tellin' the truth. Wouldn't you agree, Mr. Witherspoon?"

"Yes, sir," said Spoon, sounding like what I suspected gunner's mate Arcus Witherspoon's response to his gunnery chief would have been. Sober faced, Spoon stepped over to the flatbed's tote-all, pulled back the lid, and extracted a .30-'06. Wide eyed and with my mouth agape, I watched him sight the rifle in on one of the idling road grader's front tires and pull the trigger. The punctured tire hissed as the air oozed out of it. When Spoon quickly took out two more tires, the two men inside the cab crouched to the floor while the startled man in coveralls and his balding friend raced for the cover of a stand of nearby scrub oak.

As quickly as it had begun, the shooting stopped, and Spoon, his expression unchanged, placed the .30-'06 back in the tote-all. Offering my dad a two-fingered salute, he said, "Think we're done."

"Now, get the hell outta here, all of you," my dad yelled across the fence. "And take whatever beefed-up lies you're gonna tell Koffman—or whoever the hell pays your wages—with you."

Suddenly looking as if he'd forgotten to say something important, as the two men in the road grader rose from their hiding places on the floor and jumped from the cab and all four men raced for a nearby pickup, he yelled, "Don't any of you sons of bitches ever cross my land again without my permission. You hear me?"

By then all four men were in the pickup and the truck's engine roared to a start. The rear tires kicked up a spray of dirt and gravel as the truck made a tight circle and sped away across a sagebrush flat before heading up a grade that led back to Willard Johnson's headquarters.

I took in the still-deadly serious looks on the faces of my dad and Spoon. It was easy to see that there'd been no enjoyment for either of them in what they'd just done. In fact, from the way Spoon slowly eased himself off the flatbed and my dad shook his head as he waved me toward him, I knew they had concurred on how to handle things at Four Corners long before they'd arrived.

Uncertain what tone to take as I approached the flatbed and watched my dad and Spoon stare up at the sun as if it might offer them redemption, I said, "Looks like we've got 'em on the run."

My dad remained silent, never altering his parade-rest stance. It was Spoon who finally spoke up. "For now, TJ—for now."

Somber and silent, we headed for home.

By suppertime everyone in the Willow Creek valley knew what had happened at Four Corners that noon, largely because Sheriff Woodson, after an investigative trip to the site of the incident, had made a point of stopping by every ranch in the valley to inform the owners that the infuriated and lawsuit-minded Ed Koffman was threatening to sue every valley rancher for conspiratory life-threatening activities and threatening as well to have Woodson removed from his job, claiming that the sheriff's laissez-faire attitude encouraged vigilantism.

The sheriff stopped by our ranch last for an interrogation that lasted an hour and ended by telling us that if he had to deal with any more armed confrontations in our valley, he'd make certain someone spent time in jail. He grilled Spoon and my dad about the Four Corners incident for most of that time, suggesting all the while that their account of what had happened didn't jibe with those of the people from Acota. Fortunately, Ricky Peterson was there to remind the sheriff that what had happened at Four Corners could be corroborated by a third party, someone other than Spoon, my dad, or an Acota employee: me. When the sheriff pointed his interrogation my way, I reminded him, following Ricky's advice, that no party on either side had been injured and that the only damages incurred had been to property.

When the sheriff steered his questioning in the direction of possible assault-with-a-deadly-weapon charges against Spoon, I informed him that our property, which had been trespassed upon and contaminated by a fuel spill, had suffered a far more serious environmental transgression than damage to a few road-grader tires. Skeptical that I was offering him an opinion that was more Ricky's than my own, the sheriff drove out to Four Corners for the second time that day a little before sunset to complete his investigation, insisting that we all stay at the house until he returned. He returned an hour and a half later in darkness, Polaroid camera and color photos in hand. The dozen photos he'd taken showed the scores of tire tracks that Acota's heavy equipment had left on our land, the telltale thirty-yard-long fuel spill leading down to our gas seep, and the road grader's three flat tires.

Thumbing through the color prints with everyone gathered in the living room, the sheriff turned to me. "I'm gonna ask you again, TJ: did you see Spoon level a rifle at anyone?"

"No," I said emphatically.

He handed me several of the photos. "And the tire tracks and the fuel spill in the photographs were there when you arrived on the scene?"

"Yes."

"Quit pressing the boy, Cain. How the hell do you think those tracks could've gotten there without Acota crossing us? This is idiotic," my dad bellowed, resisting my mom's attempt to rein him in by tugging at his shirtsleeve.

"I'm not talking to you, Bill," Woodson said, turning his attention to Spoon. "And Mr. Witherspoon...," he began, sounding as if he was again going to light into Spoon.

"You don't have to respond to any questions here," Ricky said, inching forward in his chair toward Spoon.

"Don't matter," Spoon said confidently. "I didn't shoot nobody."

"Maybe you didn't," said Woodson. "But then again, you are a convicted felon, and you were out there at Four Corners firing a rifle with people in the possible line of fire."

Spoon glanced at Ricky for guidance.

"And the inference here is just what, Sheriff?" Ricky asked.

"My inference, counselor, is that I've now had two instances in the space of a month where Spoon's pulled a weapon on someone. That's real troublesome to me. Parole violation troublesome."

"I can assure you that Mr. Witherspoon met his parole obligations a long time ago, Sheriff."

"So you say. But just to be on the safe side, I'm thinkin' I should run the issue by the folks back in Ohio one more time." The sheriff flashed us all a smile that as much as said, *Maybe this time I'll get the answer I want.* "Wouldn't want to end up coddling a parole violator," he added before turning his attention back to Spoon.

"In the meantime, Mr. Witherspoon, I've got a directive for you. Don't even think about ever brandishing another weapon in these parts. If you need to kill a rattlesnake, use a shovel. You see a grizzly bear, take off in the opposite direction. You get a taste for wild game, think of the Golden Arches. You got me?"

Spoon nodded, never diverting his eyes from the sheriff's.

The sheriff glanced at my dad. "We're two for two down at Four Corners, Bill. The third time's a charm, so there best not be one." He rose, looked at my mom, and said, "Marva, I'll be lookin' at you to help these men of yours keep a lid on it."

"I'll do what I can, Harvey, but there's no love lost between me and Acota either." Ricky flashed my mom a look that said, *Marva, you've said enough*, but the look came too late. She was already wound up. "There's one thing you can make certain of, Harvey. If Acota comes back out here trespassing, I'll make sure the shots I fire won't be at their tires."

"Women aren't immune to jail time, Marva."

"Doesn't worry me in the least," my mom said, rising to escort the sheriff to the door.

At the doorway the sheriff stopped and turned back to face the rest of us. "Sure hope you take my message to heart, gentlemen." Grabbing his hat from the peg he'd tossed it onto earlier and with a smile for my mom, he left.

My mom watched him walk down the driveway to his car before turning back to us. "You heard the sheriff," she said. "It's best behavior for the lot of you. As for me, I'm loading up my 12-gauge and keeping it handy." There wasn't one hint of jocularity in her voice.

Twenty

I should have guessed that something was wrong when a week after Sheriff Woodson's visit, and on the heels of an early fall six-inch snow, I overheard Mom tell Dad, as she cleared the breakfast dishes and I prepared to leave, that Spoon hadn't shown up for a meeting he'd scheduled with Harriet Rankin at the Hardin library the previous evening. Harriet, she said, had called that morning, concerned that something might have happened to Spoon—or, even worse, that he might have simply taken off.

Convinced that Spoon wouldn't leave us twisting in the wind to work the ranch and battle Acota by ourselves, I was relieved when Spoon showed up in the machine shop shortly after breakfast, where my dad and I were busy greasing the shipping scales that my grandfather had set in place fifty years earlier. Looking annoyed, he announced, "They're crossin' you again, Bill, I'm sure of it. Had a feelin' about it mosta last night and all this mornin'."

My dad peered up from where he was lying flat on his back, squeezed beneath the scale's gear housing. Grease gun in hand and looking worn out, he said, "Maybe we should just let 'em."

"You sure?" Spoon asked. His breath curled out in the cold, still air as if to punctuate the question. "I'm thinkin' Acota's out there bent on establishin' a right-of-way. I've had

Harriet studyin' the subject. Gettin' a right-of-way established for mineral extraction would be pretty simple for them, accordin' to her, especially since you've let Willard use that dried-up-creekbed access of yours leadin' down to Four Corners for years. When you look at Acota's alternative to crossin' you to get at what they're after, which would be to come around the backside of Willard's and then across federal lands, I'm bettin' their strategy is to jump in bed with the feds and get a shared creekbed easement across you. They could claim that the two-mile trek around Willard's perimeter would cause enough ecological and endangered-species habitat damage to adjacent federal lands to warrant a shortcut. One you been sharin' with Willard all along. All they'd need would be a sympathetic judge, a county commissioner lookin' to feather his nest or put a bulge in his wallet, or some environmental wacko BLM suck-up to buy in, and bingo, you're done."

"I've heard the same argument already from Ricky," my dad said, setting aside his grease gun and wiping a half-dollar-sized dollop of grease off his right arm with a shop rag. "He says it would take Acota years to prove longtime joint usage of that creekbed access and even longer to establish potential damage to federal lands. His take is that Acota would end up wasting one hell of a lot of precious time and money."

Spoon shook his head. "Not accordin' to Harriet. Her and Edith Carthard over at the county clerk's office claim that what Acota's really lookin' to establish is one of them environmentally friendly protect-the-bunny-rabbit precedents. One that'll move things along a lot faster. Twelve, fourteen months, maybe even less, accordin' to Edith, who says she's seen 'em do it before. I'm thinkin' that if they cross the right palms, they might be able to get it done."

Surprised by Spoon's pronouncement, my dad took a deep breath and frowned. "Mind tellin' me where Edith got her law degree?" He was tired of fighting, and it showed. Tired of spearheading defunct coalitions and listening to prognostications. Tired of being the dreamy-eyed idealist looking to hang on to a world where things never changed. Tugging at the glove on his left hand, he said, "For the moment, let's just let it lie. No need chargin' up Bunker Hill on a hunch. I'll talk to Ricky this evenin' and get some advice." He sounded like someone determined to convince himself of something he didn't believe.

"Okay," Spoon said, clearly disappointed.

I had the sense that Spoon was wondering where the man who'd so defiantly stood up to Acota a week earlier had gone, and I couldn't explain my dad's reluctance to follow up on Spoon's latest premonition, especially after their earlier Four Corner's stand together, other than to assume he'd simply run out of gas.

As he stood, supporting himself by the edge of the scales, Dad looked at me. His next words were almost apologetic. "Sometimes it is more important to negotiate your way out of a situation than to fight your way into one." Brushing himself off, he glanced back at the scales. "I'd say we've got this old girl in good workin' order. Wanna step up on her and check things out for me, TJ?"

I nodded, took a couple of steps over to the scale, and climbed aboard.

"No digital readouts needed here," Dad said, proudly watching the scale's vintage glassed-in weights-and-measures needle move past 170, then 180, and stop. "One eighty-two, right on the noggin," he said.

"Fightin' weight," I said with a smile, aware that the extra five pounds I was carrying was all coat and coveralls.

Returning the smile, he said, "Yeah, fightin' weight for sure," before turning and slowly walking away.

He was gone for about thirty minutes, leaving Spoon and me alone in the machine shop to catalog, rearrange, and shelve a jumbled assortment of fan belts, air filters, hoses, and several cases of oil he'd laid in for equipment maintenance jobs over the winter. Spoon shelved things as I jotted inventory numbers on a sheet of paper that my mom would later use to enter our parts and maintenance inventory into a master log book. We'd begun the inventory system at my mom's insistence several years earlier, after my dad, certain that he had a part for the half-track we used to deliver hay to stranded livestock during snowstorms, realized in the midst of a roaring blizzard that the part wasn't there. Luckily, all we lost during that blizzard was a bull and two calves, but ever since I'd had the feeling that my mom knew where every bolt and screw on the ranch happened to be.

When I glanced through the shop's only window at a thermometer tacked to the outside window frame, I noticed that the temperature had dropped from the forty-two degrees it had been when we'd started working to thirty-four. Glancing at Spoon, I asked, "Think it's gonna snow?"

"Absolutely. I can just about feel the wind and wet flakes in my face."

"Bad?"

"Bad enough, but it'll be spotty. Easy enough to predict 'cause I'm only feelin' the cold in my face, fingers, and toes." Spoon placed a box of oil filters on a shelf and, looking puzzled, turned to face me. "Whatta you think's got your pa in such a hunker-down mood?"

"Don't know. I'm thinking maybe he's just tired."

Spoon nudged the oil filters to the back of the shelf and nodded in agreement.

"Maybe he'll have more fight in him tomorrow," I said. My breath turned into a megaphone of mist as the double doors to the machine shop rolled open.

My mom stood in the doorway. A curtain of light snow drifted down behind her, and she looked confused. She was wearing a pair of old roping boots that she'd first worn years ago when she and Harriet Rankin, who'd been raised on a sheep ranch outside Bozeman, had won the women's team roping event at the Big Horn County Fair. Looking past Spoon directly at me, she said, "Your dad told me the two of you were out here. He's dragging real bad, TJ. Want to tell me what's got him moping?"

Hesitant to discuss our earlier conversation, I said, "Afraid I don't really know."

"Well, I can tell you this. He's shuffling around the house like a man who just lost his best horse." Finally she looked at Spoon. "You got any idea what the problem is, Spoon?"

"I think he's worried about the future, Mrs. D."

"That's an odd sort of worry." She glanced over her shoulder toward the delicate flakes of falling snow. "What makes you think that?"

"Instincts," Spoon said, wrapping the word around an insightful smile. "I'm thinkin' he's tired of shadow-boxin' with the past and worried as heck about the future."

"Could be," Mom said. "I've always found it best to live in the present myself."

Spoon responded after a lengthy silence. "I don't want ya to take this the wrong way, Mrs. D., and I sure don't wanna undercut your husband, but I got a real strong feelin' we've got a problem brewin' out at Four Corners right this minute. Had it all day."

"Which would be?"

When Spoon glanced briefly in my direction, cleared his throat, and peered past my mom toward the falling snow, I knew he was concerned about revealing a confidence. "Them Acota folks are back, no question about it, and they're movin' their equipment across your property, forgin' themselves a permanent access," he said finally. "Let 'em keep at it, and trust me, they'll break ya for sure."

"What makes you so certain?" Mom asked.

"Just one of them feelin's I get from time to time."

"And you've told Bill?"

Spoon and I nodded in unison.

Mom stared into space, looking momentarily lost. "Well, at least now I've got myself an answer for Bill's behavior. Bottom line is the man's worried. Acota's probably out there putting it to us this very second, and he's got TJ trucking off to college in a few months with no blood kin around here to help him run the place but me. There's a chance there won't be a ranch left at all."

"I can stay," I blurted out. "And Spoon's gonna be here."

"You're not staying anywhere." My mom's eyes narrowed, and the determined look on her face told me it was not a time to argue. "You're going off to Missoula, TJ Darley. As for Spoon, there's no requirement on his part to make this his fight. How serious is the situation at Four Corners, anyway?" she asked Spoon.

"Serious enough that I'm thinkin' somebody needs to send Acota a message once and for all." There wasn't one hint of concern in Spoon's voice that his premonition might be off the mark.

"How would you handle things?" Mom asked.

"I'd confront 'em straight up," Spoon said without hesitation.

"Even in the face of Sheriff Woodson's orders?"

"Yep."

"And what if you're wrong? What if there's nothing out there at Four Corners waiting on us but a blizzard?"

"Then we'da had ourselves a nice wet ride in the snow," said Spoon, who seemed to sense that my mom was primed right then and there to take some immediate course of action.

"What's your take, TJ?" she asked.

"I say we go and check things out."

"And face the sheriff's wrath and maybe Acota's lawyers?"

"Yes."

Mom looked at Spoon, shook her head, and smiled. "Easy to tell that unlike his mom, my son's never spent time in jail." She forced back a snicker before offering an explanation. "Back in my New York days, we dancers had our share of artist guild problems. Union problems that caused a few nonunion hard-liners like me to spend a night or two in jail. That's something the three of us can talk about later, after we come back from Four Corners. TJ, why don't you fuel up one of the vehicles? We're going for a ride."

"Where's Dad?" I asked, full of concern. "He'll stop us for sure."

"He saddled Smokey a little before the front moved in and took off. Told me he was headed out to make sure the west-side irrigation ditch headgate was drained so it wouldn't freeze up with this snow and give us fits next spring."

"He'll be mad as heck that we took off for Four Corners without him," I said.

"He's been mad before," Mom said with a wink. "And TJ, we might as well take the flatbed. No reason in the world we should head out to Four Corners unarmed."

△ △ △

I'd never paid much attention to the fact that the heavy-duty shocks on the flatbed made the truck ride like what I suspected a World War II troop transport might have felt like, but as we jarred our way toward Four Corners in the snow and I glanced in the truck's sideview mirror and watched our ranch house disappear behind a bank of fog, I wondered if we were doing the right thing. After a few minutes of bumping along, Spoon said, staring straight ahead through the windshield, "Looks like the snow's lettin' up."

Squeezed uncomfortably between Spoon and me, Mom responded, "Good."

When Spoon countered, "Maybe not," I felt an immediate tightness in my throat. Pointing south, he said, "Why don't we go around? Come at 'em straight up Burn's Ditch and on ol' Willard's side of the fence."

"We'll be trespassing," Mom protested, as I turned south onto a red-clay, single-track road that was barely wet with snow.

"And you'd be right," said Spoon. "Except that you both been usin' that old Burn's Ditch trail by mutual agreement for over twenty years. It's a common-use access, accordin' to the law." There was a mischievous twinkle in Spoon's eyes. "Turnabout's fair play."

"So we're gonna loop in behind them—that is, if they're even there?" Mom asked.

"Oh, they're there," said Spoon.

The words had barely left his mouth when we all caught sight of several dark plumes of smoke rising in the distance. "Diesel exhaust," said Spoon, pointing toward the smoke.

I nodded in agreement as Mom said, "The snow's stopped."

I eased off the accelerator and eyed the dry ground around us. "Looks like it never got started out here."

"Let's pull up for a bit before we head down Burn's Ditch," said Spoon, staring up at a blanket of low-hanging clouds and then straight ahead toward the ditch. He seemed to be getting his bearings, calculating just how pinched in the truck would be as it navigated the mile-and-a-half, eight-foot-deep gully that funneled open just before reaching Four Corners.

Aware of the ditch's configuration, I said, "They'll see us coming."

"Probably," said Spoon. "But I'm thinkin' we'll catch 'em with their pants down at least halfway."

I eyed Spoon quizzically, wondering exactly what he thought the Acota people might be doing besides trespassing. When Mom asked, "What is it you think they're doing out there, Spoon?" I found myself thinking that at least the two of us were on the same page.

Spoon shook his head and for once looked dumbfounded. "Can't say for sure. It's just an itch I got. One that tells me that whoever's over at Four Corners has got a real bold streak runnin' through 'em. Bold enough to have 'em actin' out their ass." Looking embarrassed, Spoon said, "Sorry about the language, Mrs. D."

My mom smiled. "No apology necessary. Why don't we go see if we can't catch them acting out and spank their narrow butts black and blue."

A minute or so later we entered the mouth of the bumpy dry wash. A nearly cloudless sky lay ahead, and there wasn't a hint of snow on the ground. The lay of the land with the walls of Burn's Ditch still concealing us made it impossible at first for anyone down at Four

Corners to know we were approaching.

When the ditch opened up minutes later, I could see several pieces of equipment that hadn't been there during our previous confrontation with Acota: a mammoth idling earthmover spewing a mushroom of diesel exhaust skyward, two giant backhoes with ten-yard loader buckets, and one small and one large dozer. A van sat a few feet from the earthmover. All of the Acota equipment was on our land.

Spoon sized things up quickly as if he'd somehow magically seen everything in his head earlier. "Our fence is down," he said matter-of-factly.

Staring past the earthmover, I realized that a four-hundred-yard stretch of fence, which normally ran across the flat where the Acota equipment sat before angling directly down to our natural gas seep, was lying on the ground.

"Bold little weevils," my mom said, eyeing the downed fence and biting back obvious anger as I nursed the truck forward.

"They're sittin' right on us," Spoon said. "Think you better call the sheriff on the two-way, TJ."

"Nope, wait," my mom said as I slipped the truck's two-way radio receiver from its cradle. "Before we call the sheriff, why don't we see if a persuasive word or two might not get their attention?"

"You're not thinkin' of goin' down there, are you, Mrs. D.?" Spoon asked, looking as if he'd somehow made a grievous miscalculation. "I won't let you."

"Sorry, Spoon," Mom said. "But I'm the decision-making Darley here at the moment, and like it or not, we're going down to talk to whoever's operating that equipment and see if we can't get them to move it all off our land." With a determined face, she glanced at me. "Let's go, TJ."

I wanted to argue against the move but instead nosed the truck forward. As we headed directly toward the downed fence and out of the protective shadows of Burn's Ditch, I spotted someone walking from the Acota van toward the earthmover—someone sporting a Johnny Reb cap and dressed from head to toe in gray.

"Rodue," Spoon said softly.

I nodded without saying a word and glanced at my mom. There was obvious anger in her eyes as she gritted her teeth and said, "The nerve. The absolute nerve."

Twenty-One

Rodue made his way past the two backhoes toward the idling earthmover before turning to stare directly at us from behind aviator sunglasses. We were less than twenty yards from the small dozer when Spoon looked at me and said, "I'm thinkin' we should stop it right here, TJ."

Staring skyward through the windshield, Mom said, "Looks like it's going to clear up."

Spoon swung his door open, slipped out of the truck and eased himself up onto the flatbed. Within seconds, the cigar-smoking, bearded man whom we'd previously run off hopped down from behind the wheel of the smoke-spewing earthmover. He appeared to be wearing the same clothes he'd worn the day of our earlier confrontation, and if I hadn't known better, I would have sworn he was chomping on the same lit cigar.

"Stay in the truck, TJ," my mom ordered. As the man approached us, she slipped out of the truck as nimbly as a Broadway dancer and landed on a dry bed of grass that ran down to the natural gas seep.

"You're trespassing again, Mr. Rodue," my mom said, walking toward Rodue and another man who stood just in front of the earthmover.

"I don't think we are, ma'am," Rodue said politely. "In case you're unaware, your ranch and the Johnson place here share a common access." He removed his sunglasses and glanced toward Burn's Ditch. "Could be your husband never mentioned the fact to you. No surprise there. There'd be no need for you to fret over the operational side of things on a ranch." Rodue smiled, looked past me, and locked eyes with Spoon.

"I never fret, Mr. Rodue," my mom said authoritatively. "Fretting, I'm afraid, is for insecure men and little girls. But I do give advice, and the best advice I can offer you right now is to put my fence back up and move your equipment off my property."

"I'm not going to do that, ma'am." His gaze still locked on Spoon, Rodue pocketed his sunglasses. "And if your hired man up there on the flatbed pulls a weapon on Dwayne here like he did the other day, I'm afraid I'll have no choice but to respond in kind." He nodded at his cigar-chomping associate, who surprised all of us except Rodue by pulling a long-barreled revolver from the pocket of his coveralls. "My people have a right to feel safe while they're working, wouldn't you agree?" Rodue asked.

"Call the sheriff, TJ. Now!" Mom said to me with her eyes glued to the gun barrel.

As I reached for the two-way and dialed 911, I caught a glimpse of something moving our way out of the mouth of Burn's Ditch. When I realized that the rider on the horse galloping toward us was my dad, I didn't know whether to let out a sigh of relief or prepare for a shoot-out.

Seconds later the 911 operator asked over a background of static, "911, what's your emergency?"

"We've got a problem out at Willow Creek Ranch down at the Four Corners area."

"Please speak up, I can hardly hear you. Is anyone injured?"

"Nope, but we need the sheriff out here right away."

The operator barely got the words out, "I'll send...," before my two-way, its signal blocked by the surrounding hills and canyonlike Four Corners terrain, went dead. Redialing four times in quick succession without any luck, I looked up to see Smokey close the gap between the mouth of Burn's Ditch and us. Horse and rider had come upon us so rapidly that Dwayne, his gun now aimed in their direction, jabbed an index finger at them frantically. Rodue's response, an unintimidated nod, pretty much said *I see*.

Moments later my dad was on top of us. "What the hell's going on?" he yelled, pulling Smokey up short a few feet from the flatbed, dismounting, and looping the reins around one of the headache-rack uprights.

"Rodue and his friend there are trespassing," my mom said, calmly pointing to the downed section of fence.

"Damnit!" When my dad glanced up at Spoon, I realized that all hell might break loose any second. "Get in the truck with TJ, Marva," he said, his eyes fixed on Rodue, who stood some fifteen feet away. It was then that I saw the handle of a revolver, identical to Dwayne's, jutting from beneath Rodue's belt.

"Don't either of you take another step this way," my dad called out as Dwayne tossed his cigar into the wind.

When I heard the shuffle of Spoon's boots on the flatbed just behind my head and the tote-all's lid being opened, I pushed my mom down in the seat. The pump action of a shotgun being readied was the next sound I heard. Draped protectively over my mom, I took a long, deep breath—and then came the explosion. It was a ground-rocking blast so powerful that it threw my mom backward and then onto the floor and hurled me face-first into the dashboard. I felt an immediate wetness at one corner of my mouth that I knew could only be blood a split second before my lip went numb.

Smokey whinnied, and as I rose on an elbow to see him rear onto his hind legs, I realized that Spoon had been tossed to the ground.

"Marva! TJ, you okay?" my dad screamed.

Mom responded with a resolute, "Yes."

As she and I moved to get out of the truck, I nearly stepped on Spoon, who, butt on the ground and legs extended, was rubbing his left shoulder. "Think the fat boy with the cigar tossed aside one too many butts," said Spoon. "Damn fool might as wella lit a fuse straight to the gas seep."

A plume of thick black smoke rose from just beyond where Rodue and Dwayne had been standing. The grass surrounding them was on fire and Rodue was on the ground on his left side, moaning. Dwayne, who wasn't moving, was lying face down on his belly a few feet from Rodue.

I stared at the wall of smoke behind them and realized that flames were knifing out of a fifty-foot-long gouge in the earth.

"Damnit!" my dad yelled. "The idiots have triggered a goddamn coal fire! That natural gas seep's nothin' but a superhighway straight down to a sea of underground coal. Better get 911 on the two-way, Marva. We're gonna need help!"

Mom said, "It's not working!" Her eyes were as wide as I think I'd ever seen them as she choked out the words.

"Well, keep tryin', and tell 'em we need Fire and Rescue out here this second." Eyeing the fire, sizing up how he might tackle putting it out, he walked over to Spoon, helped him to his feet, and asked in a rush, "How you doin', Spoon?"

"Think I may've separated my left shoulder. But everything else seems intact." Spoon patted himself down with his right hand, looking pleased that he was all there.

"TJ, you sure you're okay?" Dad asked, nervously eyeing the blaze.

"I'm fine," I said, ignoring my numb lip, trying my best to erase any panic in my voice. More dazed than nervous or even scared, my mouth went bone dry.

Dad stared at the roaring blaze, then back at Rodue. "Guess we best check on Rodue and his buddy," he said, motioning for Spoon and me to follow him downhill. Eyeing my mom, he said, "Marva, stay on that two-way."

As we raced downhill, I could feel myself trembling. Just before we reached Rodue, I had the sudden urge to throw up.

Rodue, who'd been thrown fifteen feet from where he'd stood before the blast, was barely conscious. My dad and I propped him up as Spoon ran to check on Dwayne. When Spoon looked back at us and shook his head, I knew Dwayne was dead.

Spoon and my dad exchanged brief looks that said *Been here before*, and when Dad shouted, "Marva!" he might as well have been back on the battlegrounds of Korea shouting, "Medic!" As Spoon pulled Rodue out of the path of the encroaching grass fire, I had the sense that one of the most idyllic places I'd ever known had become a battlefield.

Only when my mom ran toward us, shouting, "Got through to 911! Help's on the way," did I momentarily stop trembling.

"Great," Dad said, turning his attention to Rodue. "You okay, Rodue?"

Rodue's response was a guttural, "Aaaahhh."

Dad checked Rodue's pulse, then examined his pupils. The only sense I had that Dad might have been nervous were the beads of sweat peppering his forehead. "I'm pretty sure he's got a concussion, but he's breathin'." Glancing up at my mom, he said, "Stay here with him 'til someone from Fire and Rescue or Sheriff Woodson gets here. Keep him talkin' and conscious, no matter what. Dance for him if you have to, Marva, but keep him awake."

"Okay," Mom said, kneeling to slip in behind Rodue and take over for Dad. Her face was beet red, her hands absolutely pale, and I could tell from the way she was breathing, taking quick gulps of air, that she was at least as nervous as me.

"We're gonna have to put that fire out before it gets any kind of toehold," Dad said, coughing from the smoke. He glanced around at the cache of heavy equipment before standing and eyeing each piece one by one. I could almost see the Seabee wheels turning in his head. Rubbing his hands together expectantly, he said, "Spoon, I want you on one of the backhoes." He looked at me. "TJ, think you can handle that little dozer with the muddy blade over there?"

"Yes."

"Good. I'll work the other backhoe. We're gonna trench us out enough dirt to suffocate that fire."

"What if we can't?" I asked. I could feel my heart thumping as I asked.

Dad winked and flashed me a look of pure confidence. "Don't worry. We can."

Beckoning Spoon and me to come closer and looking not the least bit apprehensive, he said, "Spoon and I'll trench out and berm up as much dirt as we can with the backhoes, ten feet or so on this side of the mouth of the fire. We'll build up a berm that's five feet high and forty or fifty feet long, then either dump or doze it into the crevice and down on the fire. We might have to open up the mouth just a bit in the end; we'll just have to see." He glanced toward a fire that was now burning so hot that my clothes had started to stick to me.

As I watched plumes of fire and smoke erupt from the gouge in the earth, I asked, coughing and wheezing from the fumes, "What about things caving in? If you open up the mouth of the fire, I mean?"

"It's a possibility," Dad said. His words were almost serene. "But we got no other choice."

"One last thing, TJ," he said, eyeing the fire pensively. "If you see the ground between me and Spoon and the mouth of that fire move the least little bit, you lay on the horn of that dozer you'll be nursemaidin'. That'll be our signal to move back."

"Okay," I said, trying my best to hide the fact that I was shaking again.

"Then let's get at it." My dad glanced at Spoon. "You're the one in the predictin' business. How do you measure our chances?"

"'Bout fifty-fifty," said Spoon, coughing and rubbing his eyes. "But since we've got a lucky charm here in TJ, I'd say we might rate just a tad better. Bottom line is, no matter the game, fifty-one to forty-nine generally wins."

I looked at my dad and saw the same proud look in his eyes that always surfaced when he talked about Jimmy. There could be no mistaking that at the moment that look was meant for me.

"And TJ, no matter what you do, stay back from the mouth of that fire, you hear me?"

My feet and hands felt numb as I nodded and glanced toward where my mom was tending to Rodue. She'd propped him up against the tree, and he wasn't moving. I glanced down at my trembling hands, momentarily lost on an imaginary battlefield until I heard the two backhoes begin to crunch their way toward the fire. Still trembling, I ran toward the dozer to carry my share of the load.

Twenty-Two

My dad's heavy-equipment-handling skills had been honed during his time as a Seabee. Where Spoon's skills had come from, I didn't know for sure. But from the time Spoon first arrived on the ranch and landed the job with his all-night hay-cutting marathon to the time I'd helped him construct the levee that guaranteed our annual hay crop, I'd realized he was the kind of person who mastered just about everything by jumping headlong into it.

He and my dad had been digging and moving dirt for a good fifteen minutes while I sat with my right palm nervously planted on the dozer's horn, dripping sweat and choking on smoke. When my dad leaned out of his cab and shouted over the roar of the fire and the groan of diesel engines, "TJ, get that dozer of yours a little closer if you can and line it up parallel to the fire," I moved the dozer twenty feet closer to the fire and prayed.

Dad and Spoon, who'd initially positioned themselves at opposite ends of the fiery crevice, were working their way toward the middle. Although the fire was so intense I thought their tires might melt, both machines were still moving as they scooped up bucket after bucket of soil and dropped it at the edge of the crevice. I watched them dig and dump and dig and dump until there was a five-foot-high, four-foot-wide berm of dirt stretching almost the entire length of the crevice.

From thirty feet away the fire's intensity was so great that the hair in my nostrils seemed to be on fire. From Dad and Spoon's vantage points, fifteen feet closer, I imagined it was suffocating. But neither man slowed his pace as they marched their machines closer and closer to one another.

They were less than two car lengths apart when I heard a loud, heart-stopping pop that sounded like a tree limb breaking. When I realized the noise had been the windshield of Spoon's backhoe exploding, I mouthed, "Shit." As both backhoes, their bucket arms nearly kissing, dropped their last loads of dirt and headed away from the fire, I could see that my dad's rear tires were smoldering. The nauseating smell of burning rubber quickly filled the air as the canted backhoe wobbled toward me.

As the two damaged pieces of equipment lumbered my way, I had the sudden strange sense that both men had retreated from similar hellholes before. When my dad pulled his backhoe to a stop a few feet from me, I could see that his face had been seared a dark, apple-butter brown. Absent a protective windshield, Spoon's face had fared worse. His eyebrows were singed, his left cheek was charred, and a shotgun spray of burn holes peppered the crown of his Stetson. Seemingly oblivious to his burns and with his injured arm hanging loosely at his side, Spoon jumped from his backhoe. Side by side, he and my dad raced in my direction.

As Spoon climbed up onto a dozer track and into my cab, the smell of burning hair filled the air, and I realized that the hair on both of his arms was completely gone. When he yelled, "Hop out, TJ," I didn't budge. "TJ, get out!" he screamed. "I gotta use this thing to bury that fire."

Shouting no, I watched my dad climb into the cab of the second, larger dozer about thirty feet away. When he waved for Spoon to move out, I was still sitting at Spoon's side.

"Damnit, TJ! You could get killed," Spoon grumbled, taking over the dozer's controls.

"So could you. Let's go."

Spoon shook his head and nosed the dozer forward. Running parallel to and less than the width of a car from my dad, we headed for the center of the berm and the crevice.

"Sure hope your pa's right about puttin' this s-o-b out," said Spoon. "I ain't doin' nothin' but followin' his lead."

Coughing and wheezing, I glanced across the gap between the two dozers. As I watched my dad maneuver his machine into place, I wondered if we'd succeed.

As we pushed the first load of dirt over the lip of the crevice and down onto the fire, I thought I heard the wail of sirens in the distance. When the two dozers backed away from the fire and as Spoon and Dad each took more acute angles on the berm in preparation for delivering a second payload, I realized that the sounds were for real. Two red and white pumper trucks out of Hardin were headed our way. Rather than feeling a sense of relief, however, I felt what could only be described as panic. Panic brought on by the fact that I knew Sheriff Woodson couldn't be far behind.

△ △ △

For the next thirty minutes my dad and Spoon, running side by side, dozed blade after blade of dirt down onto the stubborn fire. In that same space of time, half a dozen county firefighters came to our aid, but their powerful streams of water only turned the fire into a geyser of ash, flames, and mud. Even in the face of calls from the firefighters to back off, Spoon and my dad never stopped. With each new mountain of dirt he'd doze onto the fire, Spoon would look at me as he backed the machine away and say the same thing: "It's now or never, TJ. Just like Elvis always said."

During one of our assaults, amazed by Spoon's skill at the controls of the dozer, I shouted, "Were you ever a Seabee?"

"Nope," he yelled above the crackle of the fire and engine roar before taking a quick gulp of air. "Never ran anythin' but a machine gun durin' 'Nam. But Bertha and I covered for some Seabees who were rebuildin' bridges a few times. Tough bunch of buggers, them Seabees. No question," he said, taking a new angle on the berm.

When my dad yelled, "Spoon, squeeze your damn dozer over here next to mine and this hot spot," Spoon grinned and said, "See what I mean?"

Spoon dozed a couple of loads of dirt onto the hot spot before he and my dad worked for the next five minutes to plug up the far south end of the crevice. Singed and sucking in sulfurous air, we worked until Dad, waving us off, pushed a final blade of dirt down onto the smoke-billowing gap in the earth. The gap no longer spewed flames. He sat there for a moment before backing off. He brought the dozer to a stop, eased out of his cab onto the step-up, and yelled, "I'm thinkin' we can shut 'em down now, Spoon."

I listened to the earth pop and crackle for a few seconds before, following Spoon's lead, I jumped from the dozer and trotted with him toward my dad. We'd just about reached him when I saw my mom running toward us. All of our eyebrows were gone by then, and to a man we were covered from head to toe with a papier-mâché coat of gray ash. Mom hugged my dad tightly before reaching around him to squeeze both Spoon's hand and mine in hers. "It's out, it's out," she said, teary eyed.

"For now. Or it's still burning underground," my dad said, looking back toward the smoldering crevice. "We'll just have to wait and see."

Mom stepped back, looked us each up and down, and shook her head. "The three of you look like you've been in a war."

As we walked down the hill toward where I could see Sheriff Woodson standing, I asked her, "What happened to Rodue?"

"They took him to Hardin to try and stabilize him. If they can't, they're going to airlift him to Bozeman. The paramedics who hauled him off said he had a concussion and maybe even a fractured skull. Claimed it was the same kind of injury you'd get from a grenade exploding. Lucky he's not dead is what they said."

The looks on Spoon's and my dad's faces were suddenly mirror images as they eyed one another as if to say, *We know.*

As we continued toward the Four Corners survey pin, my mom let out an exhausted sigh that as much as said, *I've had enough.* A few feet from the pin, twirling his smoke-covered Stetson in one hand, stood Sheriff Woodson. "Nice work you did on that fire," he said to no one in particular. "Guess it's one time you're thankful for your navy stint, huh, Bill?"

Scrutinizing Spoon, he said, "Were you a Seabee too, Witherspoon?"

"Nope. A .50-caliber machine gunner."

"I see." Woodson slipped his hat on and said, "Afraid we need to talk, Bill."

Ignoring Woodson and turning his attention to Spoon, my dad asked, "How's the arm?"

"Think I got myself a minor shoulder separation. But it works."

"Did you hear me, Bill?" asked the sheriff.

"I heard you, Cain," Dad said, stepping over to check Spoon's injury. "And I'll get to you as soon as you get a paramedic over here to have a look at Spoon."

The sheriff waved at a paramedic who was seated on the hood of an ambulance about twenty-five yards away. "Got an injured man for you to tend to, Lonnie," he yelled. The paramedic jumped to the ground, grabbed his gear, and rushed our way.

"Soon as your hired man's tended to, we'll talk, Bill," said the sheriff.

"Absolutely," my dad said, flashing Spoon a supportive grin. "Absolutely." He placed his hand on Spoon's shoulder and they shared a strong silent glance and then a smile.

△ △ △

We did talk, all of us, and not just at the fire scene. We talked there, and at the mouth of Burn's Ditch, where the sheriff had us explain to him in detail how everything had unfolded, and finally, hours later, at the sheriff's insistence, on the front porch of our house. We talked about everything from trespassing to landowners' rights, stripmining to underground coal fires. Eventually we even discussed Dwayne James, the cigar-smoking dead man who'd started the fire.

We talked about waging battles and winning wars, about early Montana landgrabs and landgrabs back in Ohio, and when we were done, exhausted from the sheriff's grilling and still caked from head to toe with soot and ash, Sheriff Woodson, satisfied at least for the moment that he'd gotten to the bottom of what had happened at Four Corners, got up and left.

As we watched the taillights of his vehicle disappear in the night, my dad turned to Mom and asked, "Think he's satisfied?"

"As satisfied as the man who's still got a couple of missing pieces to a jigsaw puzzle can be," she said.

"Think he'll leave you alone now?" Spoon asked in a voice that had a worrisome, unsettling ring of finality to it.

"More than likely," my dad said.

With his left arm in a sling, Spoon brushed a thin layer of mud from one leg of his jeans with his right arm. "Good, 'cause I'm callin' it a day."

"Me too. And a night as well," Dad said with a quick handshake. "We'll start over in the morning."

Spoon nodded and without answering rose and walked across the porch, down the steps, and down the drive to disappear into the darkness. When I couldn't see him any longer, a sudden sense of loss and a strange sadness overpowered me. It was a feeling I imagined Spoon had experienced scores of times. I couldn't explain where the feeling had come from or why exactly it had descended on me at that moment. All I knew was that it was there, gripping me, refusing to let me go, leading me in a direction I clearly didn't want to go. I wondered if what I was feeling would linger or whether it would turn out to be only momentarily unsettling. My mom would have called it a premonition. Dad, at least now, a reasonable hunch. Deep down I knew, however, as I stared into the darkness, exactly what it was that I was feeling—recognized it for every bit of what it was. I could almost see Spoon spelling the word *charm* out in midair as I struggled with the knowledge that by the next day's sunset, Spoon would be gone.

◁ ◁ ◁

I didn't prod Spoon about his plans, nor did I discuss my premonition with him the next day as we worked side by side, setting fence posts in a pasture we used for yearling bulls in the spring. When Ricky Peterson stopped by at lunch to inform everyone that because a subsidence fire had started on our land he'd more than likely be able to get a permanent injunction against mining on our property forever, Spoon seemed elated.

I didn't say a word about my suspicions when Spoon excused himself from our dinner table that evening to head for his tack room quarters, claiming he needed to get something Harriet had given him for Mom. When he hadn't returned fifteen minutes later for his favorite dessert of peach cobbler and homemade vanilla-bean ice cream, Mom insisted that I go check on him. As I walked slowly and sadly toward the tack room, the sun had begun to set. The air was cold and clear and still, and I could hear coyote pups yelping in the distance.

The instant I pushed open the door to the tack room, a hollowness overcame me. As I surveyed the room and drank in the familiar surroundings—the saddle blankets and the boots, the neatly arranged rugs, even Malcolm— I knew that Spoon had packed his belongings and was gone.

I slowly walked that room from corner to corner, not once or twice but three gut-wrenching times, fighting back tears all the while. Choking back my sorrow, I walked to the middle of the room, where the final ebbing rays of the sun beamed through the only window to form a muted burnt orange square on the century-old heart-pine floor. It was then that I saw them. Sitting right in the middle of the floor, caked with mud and soot and ash from the previous day's fire, heels clicked together in some strange terminal salute, were Spoon's boots. Standing at attention, the boots stared up at me in the sunlight as if Spoon were still wearing them.

I walked over, picked up one boot, and thought about that night more than a year earlier when we'd shared miniature tenths of Bacardi and told each other who we were. Thought about how Spoon had rescued that very pair of boots from a discard pile and for the first time told me about his gift.

I picked up the other boot and pressed both of them tightly to my chest. The only thing I could think of, the one thing I could see as I blinked back tears, was the distant shadow of the part-Indian, part-black clairvoyant cowboy who'd once said to me, "Shoes can be excess baggage when a man's in a hurry."

Twenty-Three

I never, except in a roundabout way, heard from or saw Spoon again. A month to the day after we put out the fire at Four Corners, Harriet Rankin dropped by the ranch to let us know she'd received a postcard from Spoon. The card, which bore a Washington State postmark, had been neatly printed in Spoon's hand. He mentioned that he was in the high timber country north of Spokane in the Colville National Forest searching out a new lead that he was certain would finally take him to his roots, and that he knew things were just fine at Willow Creek. He'd signed the card with a simple *S*.

Spoon was right. Things were fine at Willow Creek. The fire at Four Corners had garnered not simply the state but the federal government's attention, triggering exactly the opposite of what higher-ups at Acota had probably wanted. For six weeks after the fire, folks from the Bureau of Land Management, the US Forest Service, the Montana Department of Natural Resources and Conservation, the Fish, Wildlife and Parks Department, and the US Geological Survey, along with high-minded and somewhat arrogant folks from the Environmental Protection Agency, mine safety, and other branches of government I barely knew existed, swarmed down on us like locusts. Seismologists claimed that the underground fire was out but added the caveat that they couldn't be certain.

When the authorities were done poking, prodding, insinuating, judging, pontificating, and gesticulating, word came down from the Montana governor's office that there'd be no more coal mining in the Willow Creek valley during my lifetime, and although the words of bureaucrats and politicians take the long way to heaven, as my dad was fond of saying, I had the sense that strip-mining in our valley was indeed dead.

Winter settled in hard, and when December fifteenth rolled around, the last day a room-and-board deposit would assure me a dorm room at the University of Montana, my dad and I were busy trailing fifty head of late-weight-gain steers back to headquarters to be shipped out the next day.

As I watched Cody nip incessantly at a lagging steer's heels, doing instinctively what he'd been bred and trained to do, my thoughts turned to Spoon. Glancing over at my dad, who sat astride Smokey, looking for all the world like a man bred to exactly what he was doing, I said in as firm and assured a voice as I suspect I ever had, "Don't think I'll be going off to Missoula next month. I'm thinking the best thing for me is to stay right here alongside you and work this land." When I relaxed back in my saddle, it seemed that a lingering burden had finally lifted from me.

It wasn't my dad's brief, deadpan response but his long, satisfied smile that surprised me. He never said, "I'm happy" or "You're doing the right thing" or "You're making a bad decision." Nor did he offer a single platitude or one ounce of homespun wisdom. His only words were, "Your mom will be disappointed," which he followed up with a question: "Mind tellin' me what brought you to your decision?"

I didn't answer immediately. Instead, I looked around at the wide expanse of partially snow-covered ground surrounding me and off into the distance toward the snowcapped Rosebud Mountains. Spoon remained at the forefront of my mind as I thought through what some people in our valley were saying about him now that he was gone. Some claimed he'd been an apparition sent to save our land, that he was the one who had taken the battle to Acota and skinned its hide, and that he, rather than Bill Darley, deserved most of the credit for winning that fight. Some said he was a Medal of Honor winner who'd come to fight one last war. A few argued that he was simply a petty criminal who'd passed through on the run.

I, however, knew the truth, and when I thought about him, quick and wiry, with his hair dragging his neckline and his eyes just about searing through your skin, all I could see was my friend. A man called Spoon who had a special gift he called a charm. A gift that he used to help me and my family rescue our lives and way of life before he moved on.

The Triangle Long Bar brand, featured throughout *Spoon* and used by the Darleys, is an historic brand that dates back to the turn of the twentieth century and lives on at the author's ranch in Wyoming.

Acknowledgments

Grateful acknowledgment is made to *Writers' Forum*, in which an abbreviated and substantially different version of *Spoon* first appeared as a short story, and to The Davies Group, Publishers, who later published a longer version of *Spoon* in *Isolation and Other Stories*.

I would further like to thank Kathleen Woodley for judiciously typing the manuscript, while at the same time managing my pathology practice, and Connie Oehring and Carolyn Sobczak for offering their keen editorial eye. Finally, I would like to thank Mary Hovland, Ann Hovland-Patterson, and Emma Patterson for historical information concerning Hardin, Montana.